JOHN COON

The Crimson Reaper

Samak Press

Power is always dangerous. Power attracts
the worst and corrupts the best.

Edward Abbey

Author's Note

Power is a dangerous thing.

We see a recurring theme from ancient myths down to modern fiction. People become corrupted through seeking power. That's what drives this latest tale from Deer Falls. *The Crimson Reaper* returns to the small Colorado town I first introduced to readers in *Pandora Reborn* six years ago. Survivors from that first story must grapple with the negative effects of dark magic again while confronting a brand-new enemy bent on becoming an all-powerful being amid a quest for vengeance.

While trying to stop a powerful new adversary, Eric Olson and his mother Emily must also battle inner demons lingering from their brush with death against an ancient witch six years earlier. I hope you will enjoy following their suspenseful and terrifying journey in this new entry in the *Deer Falls Horror Series*.

I am indebted to Sandra Coon, Jimmy Blakemore, and Joshua Coon for offering constructive feedback on story and character development in earlier drafts of this novel. 100 Covers also deserves special mention and credit for the excellent cover design. — JC

Hidden eyes tracked his movements. Robb sensed their presence. Their owner stayed concealed within shadows. For now. Soon enough, an unwelcome lurker planned to reveal themselves at the exact perfect moment. A moment where they sprang into the light and, like a coiled rattlesnake, lunged to strike a death blow.

Robb refused to let his soulless enemies succeed with their plans. Surrendering to an undeserved fate was not an option.

He jammed wrinkled clothing into an open tote bag on his bed. His eyes darted over to the alarm clock on the nightstand. Damn. Only a few minutes left before those bastards caught up to him.

If he did not flee his apartment before his unseen pursuers reached the door, his odds of escaping from Denver — or surviving — suddenly grew much slimmer.

"How did they figure everything out so fast?"

His mumbled question wedged through a crack in otherwise tight lips. Robb's eyes bounced to drawn blinds covering his bedroom window. He marched over to the window and yanked on a cord controlling the blinds. They shot up the length of the window. Clouds painted with orange and red hues crowded the horizon beyond the glass. The sun had partially retreated behind those same clouds.

Darkness would soon fall.

An identical fate awaited him if he didn't hurry.

Two cars sat stationary below his window. No new vehicles appeared along the sidewalk since he last checked. Robb bit down on his lower lip, turned away from the window, and sprinted back to the black tote bag. God, he mired himself in such a huge mess this time.

Only one way out.

A loud crack and pop greeted his ears.

Robb froze.

Each breath thickened inside his throat and grew shallower. The unidentified sound came from his living room and connected to a specific action. Someone forced his front door open.

An intruder breached his apartment.

Robb shut his eyelids and deliberately worked to calm his ragged breaths. He ran his fingers through his thick brown hair. Those protection spells that flaky little witch sold to him better work. He paid a hefty sum just to gain a morsel of her knowledge. No other choice left for him except to rely on the spells.

"I know you're in here, Robb." A gruff familiar voice sliced through the silence. "Show yourself."

Robb snapped his eyes open. He licked his lips and tiptoed over to the edge of the bed. His fingers wrapped around the worn leather cover of a thick tan book, and he laid the tome inside the open tote bag. It now rested on a pair of neatly folded long-sleeve shirts.

Footsteps made their presence known outside his sealed bedroom door. Heavy breaths followed. His throat tightened like a vise as the intruder drew closer.

"Did you really think The Order wouldn't figure things out?" The familiar voice beyond his bedroom door taunted him. "I used to think you were smart. Guess I misjudged your intelligence."

Robb scowled.

The Order misjudged many things about him. Their arrogance would be their downfall.

"It's not too late," he finally said.

"Too late for what?"

"Do yourself a favor and walk away. Being their lackey won't be worth it in the end."

A haughty laugh greeted his ears.

"Is that supposed to be a threat? You sinned against the Order. They know what you did. Now their wrath will pour out upon you without restraint."

Sinned against the Order of the Crimson Thorns?

A damned lie.

Robb served The Order with boundless energy for so long. If anything, their ruling council sinned against him and held him back from reaching his true potential.

Their minds were an open book. Each page told Robb exactly how the council wanted his story to unfold. They collectively viewed him as an insignificant bug able to be squashed at a time of their choosing.

They were wrong.

Those fools were the true insects. Soon, Robb would exterminate each councilor and claim what rightfully belonged to him alone.

Their power.

He would never again submit to being their pawn.

"You can't flee to a place where The Order won't find you," his unseen adversary warned. "They'll track you from Earth to Hell better than a bloodhound."

Robb pinched his eyes shut and bowed his head. He balled one hand into a fist and pressed it against his chest. Then, he clasped the knuckles with his other hand.

Creare concha circa corpus meum.

The phrase exited from his lips in a low whisper. An energy bubble surged through him from head to toe and seeped into every pore. Robb's eyelids popped open again. A confident smile followed.

Now he felt better prepared to face whatever lay on the other side of the door.

He turned the knob and cracked the door open. Robb made deliberate movements, not wanting to escalate into a confrontation before he had a chance to size up the adversary who pursued him here.

A curly-haired man dressed in a drab gray hoodie and blue jeans stood outside the door. He raised his chin slightly and glanced over Robb's shoulder, trying to peer into the bedroom. His eyes eventually shifted back to Robb himself after a moment.

Ethan.

He should've known The Order would send Ethan here as their agent to do their dirty work.

"Wise choice. Surrender is your only path forward after everything that's transpired."

Robb glanced down at a pistol, a .44 magnum, stuffed in his hand. His eyes trailed back to Ethan's face, and he shook his head.

"A pistol? Really, Ethan?"

"Can't be too careful when it comes to you."

Now The Order considered him dangerous? Where was this concern when they butchered Geoff and turned Amy against him?

They were afraid.

They should be afraid.

"Did you think you could steal the reaper amulet without repercussions?" Ethan lectured him like an irate parent dressing down a rebellious teen. "Now you're going to return it."

"You don't have all the information." Robb opened the door. He raised his hands and made a push motion at Ethan. "You're only a nameless agent. Subject to their whims. Expendable. Listen to me — don't accept their lies as gospel truths."

"I serve the Order of the Crimson Thorns alone." Ethan bristled at his accusations of ignorance and blind obedience. "You will not sway me from my true path. My sole duty is to bring you in and let the council in their wisdom decide your fate."

His words qualified as the sort of pure drivel Robb expected a puppet of The Order to spit back at him.

"I'm sorry you feel that way." Robb let out a weary sigh. "I guess I can't reason with a man who refuses to listen to reason."

"Let's go."

"I'm not going anywhere with you."

"Then you leave me no choice."

Ethan cocked the pistol. A determined scowl deepened on his lips. Robb's eyes instinctively darted to the barrel pointed squarely at the center of his chest. His heart pounded as though struck by an invisible hammer with repeated blows.

This damned spell better work.

A bullet exited the chamber with a loud blast. Robb jammed his hands into his pockets and stood unmoving. The bullet stopped in mid-air with a sudden jolt. It plummeted to the carpet mere inches from his chest; the casing now crushed like a soda can.

Ethan stared at Robb wide-eyed. His mouth dropped open. He quickly shook his head and fired off two more shots. Neither bullet reached Robb before also plunging harmlessly to the floor, flattened in the exact manner as their predecessor.

"How … are you … doing this?" Ethan fumbled over the question while backpedaling a few steps from Robb. "You should be dead."

Robb flashed a knowing grin.

"A simple protection spell," he said. "And, obviously, also quite an effective one."

"Natural magic doesn't flow through your veins. Who cast this spell upon you?"

Robb narrowed his brown eyes. Did Ethan consider him to be an irredeemably stupid son of a bitch? Anyone who truly knew him understood he wouldn't betray his allies to The Order for the sake of saving his own skin.

Porta clausa.

Robb whipped his left hand out of his pocket and threw it forward like a pitcher releasing a fastball. Ethan turned and dashed toward the front door. It slammed in his face with ferocity, shaking the entire door jamb. He yanked on the doorknob.

The door refused to budge in either direction.

"I have more than one spell at my disposal." Robb punctuated his revelation with a brief chuckle. "You're in my realm now. How will you survive?"

Ethan kept a firm grip on the pistol, but his hand started to tremble. Fear swallowed his eyes whole, and he licked his lips.

"See, here's your dirty little secret." Robb's smile turned crooked as he drew closer again. "I'm betting you didn't bother to use a protection spell to cover your own ass before coming after me."

He lunged toward Ethan and knocked the pistol out of his hand. Robb wrestled him to the floor and tried to wrap both hands around the agent's throat. Ethan deflected his arms and scrambled to his feet.

He raced into the kitchen. Robb followed on his heels. Ethan snatched a stainless-steel pot from a green drainboard flanking the sink. He pivoted around and swung at Robb's head. The pot stopped inches short of striking his skull and vibrated as though it collided with an invisible force field.

"God, you're such an idiot."

Robb shook his head. He batted the pot out of Ethan's hand. Metal clattered against the linoleum. Heavy panicked breaths escaped from the agent's lips as he grew aware of the predicament facing him.

"If a bullet can't penetrate this protection spell, what makes you think a random pot will do the job?" Robb took pleasure in taunting Ethan. He faced a hopeless situation. "Don't you worry, though. I promise I'll end this mess right now."

He raised his other hand and pointed Ethan's pistol back at him. The agent pressed his back against the sink and raised his hands.

"Please. We can work out a deal here."

"A deal?"

"You and me. No one else needs to know. I have a family and they deserve —"

"And I don't?" Robb cocked the pistol. "The time for reasoning has passed. The Order wanted to send me a message. I'll send them a message instead."

He unloaded two bullets straight into Ethan's chest. Ethan slumped to the floor, blood oozing down his hoodie in twin parallel trails. He coughed and gagged with violence. More blood passed through grimacing lips.

Robb drew closer and stood over the dying agent.

"You're right," he said. "I took the amulet and I intend to use it."

Ethan glanced up at him, eyes widened and silently pleading for Robb to not follow through with his plans.

"I promise once I unlock its full power, I'll destroy the ruling council and take their place," Robb said. "A worthy fate for everything they've done to me."

He raised the pistol a second time.

Click.

Robb glanced down at the firearm and scowled. An empty chamber and a spent magazine.

He shrugged and tossed the pistol aside. Robb opened a drawer and drew out a butcher knife. Fluorescent light glinted off the shiny blade. Ethan shook his head and started crawling away from the sink, trying to elude a fate staring at him in his bloodied face.

He didn't succeed.

Robb jabbed the broad blade downward through his upper neck. Ethan expelled a final violent gasp and collapsed face first on the linoleum. Blood pooled under his gunshot wounds and trickled down his neck. Robb withdrew the blade again and cast the knife aside.

"Always have a backup plan," he said.

2

Plumes of dust kicked up around Eric's bike when both tires touched down on the trail again. A huge grin popped on his lips, and a triumphant yell followed. No chance anyone else executed a 180 spin on that jump as perfectly as he did. Footage from the GoPro camera mounted on his helmet would supply more than enough proof. Max, Tatiana, and Devin were all competing for second-best once again.

Eric cast his eyes side to side and quickly glanced over his shoulder. Tatiana's bike went airborne as her front tire crested over the trunk of a fallen lodgepole pine tree. Max and Devin trailed a few yards behind her. All were half a football field behind him. His grin pushed against the corners of his mouth. Eric snapped his head forward again and leaned into his handlebars. He shifted gears and dug into his pedals. His bike barreled down the winding trail, slicing through a thicket of towering pines and stout firs.

"This is too easy," he said, adding a laugh.

The trail leveled out into a flat field blanketed by uneven wild grasses. A bubbling creek carved a meandering path through the heart of the field. Eric pedaled toward a narrow wooden plank bridge supported by sturdy metal piers underneath the planks. Although the bridge crossed over the creek, no railing boxed in either side to prevent unlucky souls from plunging into chilly mountain waters below. Eric skidded to a stop a few yards beyond the bridge and turned his bike sideways. He rested on the seat and faced back toward the trail, watching his friends zip down through the same thicket of trees in succession.

Tatiana reached the bridge first. She gritted her teeth and wore a determined frown as she pedaled over the bridge. Once her back tire cleared the final plank, Tatiana let loose a celebratory shout.

"Personal record!" A satisfied smile replaced her frown. "I covered our downhill run in 13 minutes!"

She squeezed her handbrakes and slowed her pace. Eric unleashed a loud laugh when Tatiana pulled up beside him.

"Felt more like 13 hours," he scoffed. "I could have streamed every Avengers movie while I waited for you."

Tatiana rolled her eyes.

"Bullshit. You reached the bridge like two minutes before me. I'm not an idiot."

He laughed again, earning a scowl from her.

Devin sprinted across the bridge next. He edged out Max by a full minute. Both teens pulled up alongside Eric and Tatiana.

"Which trail are we hitting next?" Max asked.

Eric leaned forward on his handlebars and surveyed the meandering creek, searching for a gully where another trail crossed downstream. One with an equal or better climb to what Bobcat Creek Trail offered.

"How about Keg Hill?"

That suggestion jarred Eric to the bone as soon as it greeted his ears. He snapped his head toward Tatiana.

Keg Hill?

Not a chance in hell.

Eric wouldn't ride that trail in a million years. Not even for a million dollars. His refusal had nothing to do with the trail's length or difficulty of the upper climbs.

Keg Hill was a dark place.

"Pick another trail," he said. "Keg Hill is off limits."

Tatiana narrowed her blue eyes into a half-squint and scrunched her nose. An annoyed frown simultaneously washed over her lips.

"Who died and made you the forest cop?"

"We can't go over there. Just trust me on this."

"Why?"

"Because that's the spot where my brother and sister-in-law buried the chest."

A sarcastic laugh from Tatiana greeted his revelation.

"Oh no. Your alleged ancient witch may strike again."

"There's nothing alleged about her or what she did to my family." Eric's eyes hardened into a fierce glare. "Riding over to Keg Hill is a stupid idea. We should stay as far away from that buried chest as possible."

"I'm with Eric." Max said. "We both nearly got killed the last time someone let that witch outside of her chest."

Tatiana shrugged. She leaned forward in her seat and started pedaling away from Eric.

"Try and stop me," she said without looking back.

Devin flashed a grin and followed on her heels. Eric and Max exchanged worried glances. What exactly did Tatiana have in mind? Dismissing their experiences as an urban legend or tall tale only opened the door for an indescribable evil to strike. That ancient witch possessed enough power to end their lives without breaking a sweat.

The worst part? Christina wasn't here to help fight back this time. She and Ron hadn't lived in Deer Falls since leaving for college nearly five years ago.

Eric and Max finally caught Tatiana and Devin a quarter mile past the bottom of Keg Hill. They had followed a snaking trail to four pine trees that formed a perfect semicircle. Sweat gathered on Eric's brow and his breaths grew heavier. These were not byproducts of racing to catch his friends.

He recognized the cluster of pine trees.

Ron and Christina warned him and Max away from ever visiting this spot. It served as a permanent burial ground for the chest holding that sadistic witch. His sister-in-law feared what would happen if anyone disturbed the chest again. Neither Eric nor Max needed extra convincing to avoid Keg Hill and the surrounding vicinity. Their experiences offered enough evidence for dangers that a witch drunk on dark magic posed.

Eric glanced over at Max. The same paralyzing fear gripping him from head to toe threaded through his best friend's face.

"We have to turn back," Max struggled to conceal the tremor in his voice. "This isn't a place where we should be dicking around."

Tatiana squeezed her handbrake and coasted to a stop in front of the nearest pine tree. Devin and the others mimicked her actions. She instantly glanced over Max and rolled her eyes.

"Dude, stop being such a pussy."

"I'm not being a pussy. You're being an idiot."

"Idiot?" Tatiana narrowed her eyes again. "I'm a hell of a lot smarter than you."

She turned away and faced the pine trees again.

"What are you two so afraid of anyway?" A palpable annoyance permeated her voice. "Even if I believed your witch existed, how would I dig up the chest? It's not like any of us brought along a shovel. Not that it matters."

Tatiana's persistent skepticism only fed the creeping dread crawling up Eric's spine and spreading through the rest of his body like a spider web. Frustration seized him in equal measure. Tatiana seemed determined to prove a point to him and Max. Nothing good would come from her stubbornness.

"You don't need a shovel to bring back a witch," Eric said. "We're dealing with dark magic here."

"Dark magic?" Devin's eyes widened.

Tatiana let out a forceful sigh and followed with a sarcastic laugh.

"You three sound like the scaredy-cat twins I babysit. They're seven years old. What's your excuse?"

Eric's frown deepened.

"What I'm saying is one wrong word or phrase —"

"Just stop it, okay?" Tatiana answered Eric with a dismissive wave. "So, if I raise my hands and say, 'O' powerful ancient witch, break free from the chest binding you,' then — according to you — it will happen?"

She paused and narrowed her eyes.

"Bull. Shit."

Tatiana lifted her arms skyward during her rant. Eric's throat tightened and his heart raced at a sprinter's pace. Was her gesture deliberate or a subconscious action? Then again, such a distinction didn't matter.

She called on the witch to arise again.

A violent tremor rippled through the ground below their mountain bikes like an invisible wave. Eric tumbled off his seat and crunched down on his elbow. He winced. Broad cracks formed in the rocky soil. All four bikes toppled over amid continued shaking.

"Earthquake!" Max shouted.

He turned and crawled back toward his bike. Eric's eyes trailed away from his friend to the four pine trees. Each newly formed crack traced back to a central origin near the trees. From this spot, cracks spread out in every conceivable direction and widened with each new tremor rippling through the ground.

A dense red mist billowed through the cracks.

Eric stumbled as he tried to scramble to his feet and pick his bike off the ground. Panic threaded through the faces of his three friends as they mirrored his actions.

Mist coalesced above a broad fissure between Tatiana and the nearest tree. It formed into the outline of a young woman dressed in a flowing gown. Black swirled through red as the gown gained color and definition. Her arms and face grew sharper and solidified in a similar fashion.

"Run!" Eric screamed.

Devin scrambled to his feet first and pulled his fallen mountain bike upright. Tatiana backed up against her bike as the witch turned to face the teen. Her eyes froze on the malevolent being.

At once, the witch shot out a fully formed arm toward Devin as he hopped on his bike to flee. Hardened soil beneath him softened like quicksand. It gripped each tire and wrenched the bike frame downward. Devin tried to spring free from his seat. All four limbs refused to move.

His hands fused to the handlebars.

His feet fused to the pedals.

Devin screamed and struggled to free himself until the soil finally swallowed his body whole — permanently silencing him. Eric cupped his hand over his mouth, fighting an urge to vomit. He scrambled to his feet, searching for a way to distract the witch so he, Tatiana, and Max could survive and flee.

Another scream greeted his ears. Eric snapped his head toward Tatiana. The witch uttered a string of strange words in a guttural tone. At once, hordes of bugs sprang from the ground on all sides.

Spiders.

Ants.

Wasps.

Every insect species imaginable materialized.

Bugs converged on Tatiana as she sobbed and tried to shield her face with her hands and arms. They scurried up her limbs and swarmed over her head, consuming everything in their path.

The witch extended her arm out from her side without looking. A sickening snap followed. Max's bike crashed a second later. Eric refused to turn and confirm his best friend's death. Witnessing Tatiana and Devin die in rapid succession pushed him past his breaking point.

He was left alone to battle the witch.

Now fully formed, she wheeled around and locked eyes with Eric. Cassandra appeared identical to what he remembered from battling her inside the abandoned house six years earlier, right down to the same menacing smile. A lump formed inside his throat. Tears streamed down both cheeks.

How could he withstand such a powerful being alone?

"Your foolish friend should never have freed me," Cassandra said. "You will never get a second chance to seal me inside that wretched chest again."

Eric's fingers snapped together, forming a fist around a wooden handle. His eyes drifted downward. A steak knife rested in his hand. The serrated edge turned inward toward his chest.

"Time to finish what I started with you."

He pushed back against his wrist while Cassandra laughed. The blade inched closer and closer to plunging through fabric and flesh. His eyes snapped shut and Eric unleashed a terrified scream.

"Dude, are you okay?"

Eric's eyes blinked open again. He found himself on the ground, lying on his back. Max stood over Eric. Tatiana and Devin were a couple of steps behind Max. Concern threaded through their faces.

A horrifying thought barged into his head.

Where is Cassandra?

Eric cast his eyes to one side, and they trailed back to the other. His bike lay on its side just a few feet away from him.

No sign of the witch.

"What's going on?" Panic threaded through his question. "You're all supposed to be dead."

"Huh?" Tatiana glanced over her shoulder. Her blue eyes quickly slid back to Eric. "Riding down Bobcat Creek Trail isn't that dangerous."

Eric bolted upright and surveyed his surroundings. They were still at the bridge where the trail crossed over Bobcat Creek. He drew in a sharp breath and rubbed his hands down his cheeks.

They never rode over to Keg Hill. Cassandra remained safely locked away inside the buried chest. He had only suffered another waking nightmare.

Another hallucination.

"I saw her." Eric shook his head. "The witch. Tatiana called her forth and she slaughtered you three. She started to force me to impale myself a second time when I suddenly found myself here again."

A worried frown washed over Max's face.

"Another hallucination?" he said. "I thought you licked that problem."

"So did I," Eric said. "What happened?"

"You zoned out like my older brother when he smoked weed," Devin said. "Just kept staring over at Keg Hill. Then, suddenly, you fell off your bike seat and started screaming like an angry clown attacked you."

Eric licked his lips and ran his hands through his brown hair, locking his fingers together behind his head. This wasn't supposed to still be happening to him. After going five months without enduring an episode, he thought his mind had finally healed.

"We better head home." Tatiana extended her hand and helped Eric to his feet. "You're not in the right headspace to ride any other trails."

Eric nodded without saying a word. Going home was the sensible thing to do. Of course, he wished he didn't have to go. Once his mom learned about his latest episode, Eric would be making another trip to see that damned therapist.

3

Whenever a smile wormed across her lips, Eric cringed. His silent reaction wasn't one born out of fear or discomfort. Disgust bred his feelings.

Dr. Rainer's smile defined phony to the letter. His therapist gave off a vibe consistent with an adult who ached to wring an unruly child's neck and only held back to avoid unsavory consequences such an action promised. Eric learned enough from speaking with this woman during their past therapy sessions to not trust her motives for a second.

If he had a choice, he'd walk straight out of her office, let the door slam behind him, and never come back.

Eric didn't have a choice.

"We were making such wonderful progress," she said. "What triggered this latest episode?"

What a stupid question. Dr. Rainer knew damn well what triggered this hallucination — and all earlier ones. She just refused to face reality.

Like virtually everyone else who lived in Deer Falls.

Eric leaned forward, perched on the edge of the beige couch. He rested his elbow on his quad and pressed his hand against his forehead. An unrestrained sigh followed.

"You know exactly why this happened." Eric studied the area rug under his feet, refusing to make eye contact. "How many times do I have to repeat myself before you'll believe me?"

Silence greeted his question.

"I never lied about anything I've shared with you," he insisted, finally lifting his eyes to meet her gaze. "Why would I make that shit up?"

Dr. Rainer pushed her wire-rimmed glasses up along the bridge of her nose. She glanced down at a small legal pad. Yellow paper was partially visible from his angle on the couch and revealed several sentences scribbled in unintelligible cursive script.

"Trauma can play with our memories." His therapist refocused her gaze on him again. "Sometimes, it is easier to retreat into an elaborate personal fantasy as a coping mechanism to deal with what occurred in the real world."

She really thought he was a liar, didn't she? Eric was having none of her nonsense this time.

"Ever had a witch use magic to try to force you to impale yourself with a knife?" Eric's eyes hardened and his tone sharpened at an equal rate. "Not a life experience any middle-school kid craves. And definitely not some fucked up lie I cooked up in my head."

Dr. Rainer uncorked a brief irritated sigh.

"We both know what the police report detailed." Efforts to mask her true feelings waned in her voice. "The girl who attacked you belonged to a Denver street gang running a drug trafficking ring. No magic. No witchcraft. Just a simple old-fashioned violent criminal."

Eric buried his cheeks between his hands and his eyes darted back to the area rug. A frustrated frown graced his lips. Painting Cassandra as a mere drug runner or gangster was the real lie here. She posed a much larger threat than either scenario entailed. Cassandra possessed enough power to destroy countless people with a simple wave of her hand or through reciting a brief incantation.

Nobody in Deer Falls seemed willing to confront the truth about this town. The official story surrounding her rampage six years ago offered concrete evidence of this unwelcome truth. The mayor, the sheriff, local pastors — all parties were complicit in fabricating endless cover stories. They all buried their heads so deep in the sand, Eric wondered if any of them still remembered when they last saw sunlight.

"I want this office to be a safe space for you, Eric," Dr. Rainer said. "You can trust me. I'm here to help you. I'm truly on your side."

Eric let his hands fall to his lap and met her gaze.

"You're on my side?"

"Since day one."

"If you're on my side, then you should have no trouble believing me."

"Here's what I believe: you're crying out for help in your own way. Your subconscious mind is still struggling to cope with a pair of major traumas occurring so close together. It's a heavy burden for a young boy to endure."

Perfect.

Dr. Rainer shoved his parents' divorce right into the mix again. As if it had anything to do with what Cassandra did. Eric grew sick long ago of her attempts to associate all the shit he had endured in Deer Falls with his father deserting him, his mom, and his brother.

His old man never once set foot in this town. Just like Eric wished he never set foot inside this therapist's office. He glanced over at a wall clock and then back at Dr. Rainer. Eric crossed his arms.

"Do me a favor. Let me know when my hour is up."

His therapist flashed an uncomfortable smile and quickly snatched up the legal pad from a round table next to her chair. A pen click followed. She flipped past several older pages and scribbled down fresh notes on a blank page. Dr. Rainer probably had nothing positive to say about this session. Not that Eric cared. She could be as mad as she wanted to be. It wouldn't change anything.

He had nothing left to say to a therapist who didn't bother listening to him from the start.

* * *

The trapdoor hinge squeaked. Eric slid his eyes over to the door as it rose off the treehouse floor. An arm pushed the trapdoor against a posterior wall. His mom, Emily, poked her head through the opening.

She offered a reassuring smile.

"I thought I'd find you up here," Emily said. "Mind if I join you?"

He shook his head and beckoned his mom forward with his hand. Emily climbed through the opening and hoisted her lower body up into the treehouse. She planted herself on a beanbag chair next to the one he occupied. Eric's eyes shifted from his mom over to a flat screen TV on the opposite wall.

A frozen image of blood splattering from a bullet striking a zombie's head filled the screen. Eric made no move to resume the game. His eyes were transfixed on the zombie's contorted rotting face. The controller dangled from his hand.

"I can't go back."

Eric's subdued tone contrasted with intensifying frustration gripping him. A deepening frown crossed his lips. Surely, his mom understood nothing beneficial came from these therapy sessions?

"We don't really have a choice," Emily said. "The high school mandated therapy."

"What good does it do when my therapist won't believe anything I tell her?" Eric's eyes slid back over to his mom. "I always feel like I'm talking to a tube of toothpaste when I'm there."

Emily pivoted in her beanbag chair and faced him. She cracked a brief knowing smile.

"I feel the same way."

"So why do we keep doing it? I'm not crazy. You're not crazy. Our experiences aren't a huge lie we cooked up."

"I wouldn't believe the things we witnessed if I hadn't endured them myself." Emily's smile vanished again. She pinched her eyelids shut as if blocking her eyes from seeing Cassandra anew. "I wish I knew how to open everyone's eyes and convince them witches do exist."

The controller dropped from Eric's hand. It clattered against a wood plank. He sighed and licked his lips.

"I'm scared, Mom."

Her eyelids snapped open. Concern flooded Emily's eyes. She sprang off her chair and scooted up next to Eric on the other beanbag. Emily wrapped her arms around him in a comforting embrace.

"I know you are sweetie. So am I. I wish I knew what to do to help you feel better."

Eric mirrored her action, encircling his arms around his mom's back. He closed his eyes and rested his head against her cheek.

"I thought the hallucinations were gone for good." He fought against tears enveloping his eyes and drowning his voice. "I went so long without seeing her. Nothing I've ever tried to do to break her hold over my mind works."

"We'll find a way together."

Invisible fingers of doubt wrapped around Eric and squeezed his brain tight like an orange. His mom would never give up on him. Quitting was not part of her nature. Still, every solution they tried met with failure. Not even Christina found a way for his mind to absorb the trauma and bury it forever.

Pleas Eric made to her during a Christmas visit bounced back into his head — still as fresh in his ears as when he spoke those long-ago words. He saw himself again in his mind's eye begging his sister-in-law to cast a healing spell. A simple, yet powerful, incantation to undo the damage Cassandra inflicted on him.

Sad hazel eyes and a resigned frown told Eric she would not grant his wish.

"I can't do what you want me to do," Christina said.

She stood in the doorway to his bedroom, wearing a thick dark blue coat and snow pants. A matching scarf wrapped around her neck and a knit cap covered her head. A couple of deep brown curls poked out from either side of the cap, dipping down to mid-cheek. Christina picked the perfect attire to brave the chilly air and carve ice sculptures with Ron.

Eric sensed she'd rather be outside perfecting their new hobby than dealing with his latest internal crisis. Still, their sculptures could wait. He needed Christina to build something more important.

"I'm not asking much," Eric insisted. "Maybe you could say a few special words to make me forget I ever encountered Cassandra."

Christina's frown deepened in the corners of her lips.

"Not a chance." She shook her head. "You're asking me to do a terrible thing. I won't manipulate your mind for any reason. That's a gateway to dark magic."

"How does erasing a bad memory equal dark magic?"

"Think about it for a second. You know the answer."

"No … I really don't."

Christina's eyes shifted away from him and settled on a window above his shoulders. Eric resisted the urge to follow her lead and see what lay outside the glass. His gaze stayed fixed squarely on her worried face as he sat on the edge of his bed.

"If I mess with your memories, I'll change who you are." Her eyes trailed back down to his. "Such actions would put me on the same level as Cassandra in the end."

Her declaration stuck with Eric even as his mind brought him back to the treehouse with his mom. If Christina with all her powerful magic was unable to do anything to help him out, what solution remained to make everything better?

"Why don't we just move from this place?"

Eric's question caused his mom to pull back from their embrace. She flashed a disappointed frown.

"It's not that simple," Emily said.

"Why not?"

"I listed our house for an entire year. Barely drew flies, let alone interested buyers."

Eric hung his head and pinched his lips together. If his mom couldn't sell the place, why not do the next best thing? Find a willing tenant, collect rent, and put Deer Falls in the rear view mirror.

"Maybe we should rent this house," he said, giving life to his thoughts. "Different path. Same outcome. We get out of this goddamn town."

Eric met his mom's gaze again, searching for signs she at least seriously entertained his idea. Her sorrowful eyes told him this possibility also hit a roadblock.

"It sounds like a good idea, honey, but so much work will go into being a landlord," Emily said. "We need to find a reliable and trustworthy property manager. I don't want the constant headache of dealing with a tenant by myself. We also need to make a few repairs around here."

"So that's it? You're not even considering my idea?"

"I didn't say that."

"But that's what you're thinking."

Emily laid her hands gently on both shoulders and stared unblinking into his eyes.

"I will do my best. I promise."

Eric took his mom at her word. He imagined she would start groundwork on converting their house into a rental property before the day ended. Whatever she had to do needed to be done fast. Eric feared his mind would shatter beyond repair forever if they waited too long to move away from this place.

4

Sunlight streamed through a narrow crack where drawn curtains met. Those faint rays helped illuminate a darkened motel room. Robb perched on the edge of his bed, palms gripping his knees. His eyes were glued to a flat-screen TV mounted on a swinging fixture fastened to the opposite wall.

"Police in Denver tonight have released the identity of a victim of a brutal homicide at Lawson Park. Ethan Garvey, aged 32, was found dead on an outdoor basketball court at the park by a jogger early Thursday morning. The victim suffered multiple gunshot wounds and a stab wound."

A middle-aged woman sitting behind a news desk droned on in a serious tone as she detailed this gruesome discovery. Robb's fingers tightened around his kneecaps. He drew a sharp breath. His eyes instinctively darted from the anchor's blue blazer over to his motel room window. Did he leave any incriminating evidence behind when he staged the crime scene? Robb took great care to destroy anything capable of tracing Ethan's slaying back to him.

"A small pouch filled with marijuana was found on the body," the news anchor said. "A spokesperson for the Denver Police Department said they believe a drug deal escalated into violence. Mr. Garvey, however, had no prior history of drug use or drug-related arrests."

Robb's eyes slid back to the anchor's Botox-enhanced makeup-laden face. A satisfied grin sprouted on his lips. Of course, Ethan didn't do drugs. Anyone who met him would reach that conclusion within five minutes. He fashioned a clean enough facade to masquerade as an insufferably nice Mormon and fool everyone.

That's how The Order wanted to run things.

The ruling council demanded mental clarity from their agents. Of course, they also wanted agents single-minded enough to execute the Order's whims at any given time. Ethan also fit with the second part of that equation to perfection.

"Authorities have not yet publicly identified a suspect behind the slaying. Investigators are still piecing together a timeline of the crime and will release more information as it becomes available."

Robb snatched up the remote control at his side and clicked off the TV. A relieved sigh escaped his lips. His efforts to scrub his former apartment and dump Ethan's corpse at the park paid off.

No one saw his car arrive just after 2 am or depart a few minutes later. Such an ungodly hour was a perfect time to stage a crime scene. Any normal person would be tucked away under their blankets sawing logs while dreaming of better days.

Robb left no detail to chance upon arriving at the park. Dark clothing concealed his visibility and identity. He parked his car a safe walking distance from working streetlamps, so none revealed his license plate to a hidden camera. Once Robb scrubbed his fingerprints from Ethan's pistol and his butcher knife, he disposed of both weapons in random dumpsters at separate locations.

Only a few key tasks remained.

Disposing the bloody sheet wrapped around Ethan took top priority. The soiled fabric still lay nestled inside his trunk. Then, Robb had to find a quiet place where he could stay hidden from other agents of the Order of the Crimson Thorns. Harnessing the full power existing within the reaper amulet required gathering knowledge and showing patience. They must not be allowed to track him down before he succeeded in his plans.

"So many miles left to travel before I sleep."

Robb half-mumbled those words as he sprang off the bed. He marched over to a black tote bag resting on an ugly beige chair in the corner. His hand plunged past a pulled-back zipper and rummaged under a layer of folded shirts and rolled-up socks. Fingers locked around a pendant nestled amid assorted fabric. Robb drew out the special talisman from its hiding place and uncurled his fingers. His eyes trailed over an object requiring so much sacrifice to obtain.

Two intersecting crimson bars resembling scythe blades formed the amulet. A design that both intrigued and amused Robb. The Order of the Crimson Thorns created this symbol as a subtle act of mockery toward a primitive faith their ancient founders despised.

Teardrop sapphires adorned the blunt end of each scythe bar. Their dark blue hue offered an intentional contrast to the rest of the amulet. Robb fixed his attention on the diminutive gems.

Symbols of power and strength.

Emblems of prophecy.

Hallmarks of royalty.

He needed to unlock everything the amulet promised. It offered his only certain path to make The Order face justice for their crimes.

Geoff never deserved the fate he received.

"These are kick-ass seats!"

His brother's happy declaration rang fresh in Robb's mind as though the words greeted his ears only a moment earlier. Drab trappings of a cheap motel room faded from sight with the speed of a vanishing desert mirage. Robb found himself back in Denver — sitting inside Ball Arena next to Geoff. Four rows up from the court. Their seats put the siblings right behind the basket on the south end.

Robb turned to his brother and cracked a grin.

"You have to watch March Madness in style," he said. "This isn't the time to cheap out on nosebleed seats. Go big or go home."

Geoff nodded and returned a grateful smile.

"I owe you one. First chance I've had to watch my team in the tourney in person."

Robb's eyes slid down to Geoff's t-shirt. Gonzaga's school logo was emblazoned across the chest. His brother popped out the logo with his thumbs.

"This is the year my Zags win it all. I feel it."

"I don't know, man. I picked Kansas to cut down the nets in my bracket. Rock. Chalk. Jayhawk."

Geoff answered him with a brief chuckle.

"You always pick Kansas to win."

Robb shrugged and redirected his gaze toward the Gonzaga bench. He and Geoff watched one player after another drive to the basket while going through layup drills. The Zags' school band belted out a deafening tune only a few rows behind their seats.

Boisterous music devolved into a ringing phone. Images of Ball Arena fled from Robb. He found himself back inside the motel room, the amulet resting in his open palm. A silver chain looping through the vertical bar just above one of the sapphires dangled over the side of his pinky finger.

Robb glanced over at a small square end table where his smartphone rested. An unfamiliar number graced the lit-up screen. He gnawed on his lower lip, debating internally on whether he should answer the call, before finally snatching the phone off the table.

"Hello?"

"You can't flee forever. You belong to us. We will find you."

A peculiar gravelly voice breathed out the threat to him. Robb's cheeks grew hotter. He clenched his teeth. The mystery caller made a huge miscalculation. Their words stimulated anger rather than fear.

"You don't want to catch me." Robb's tone matched the menace from the voice on the other end. "It won't end well for you."

Silence greeted him.

Robb pulled the phone away from his ear. The screen had gone blank again — displaying only time, date, and a smattering of app icons. Not that it mattered. Any threats against him would return to the agents who made them in the most painful way imaginable.

He would see to it himself.

Robb strolled over to a compact desk in the opposite corner from the end table. He unzipped a computer bag and drew out a laptop. After plugging it in, Robb opened the computer and logged into a VPN. He pulled up a private browser window. A search engine home page appeared on screen.

"I need to find a place where I can't be found."

Robb mumbled, guarding his words as though unseen spies listened in on him talking to himself. Perhaps they were eavesdropping. The Order had a global reach. Their agents could be anywhere and take any form.

Geoff learned that hard truth in a devastating way.

Nothing seemed amiss while they watched Gonzaga escape a bracket busting upset to a double-digit seed on a last-second basket. Robb joined his brother in jumping to his feet and cheering the Zags' triumph until their voices grew hoarse. Images of the game-winning layup passed before his eyes as if unfolding in real time all over again.

Life never felt better when the clock hit zero and the horn sounded.

"What a finish!" Geoff grinned and shook his head. "I thought for sure he'd pull up for a three instead of driving all the way to the rim."

"Their defense must have thought the same thing," Robb said. "He had a clear lane to the hoop."

He followed his younger brother up the stairs and through the portal leading out to the concourse. Another first-round game tipped off in less than an hour, but Robb only bought tickets for Gonzaga's game. No worries. Getting tickets for a second-round game on Saturday wouldn't be difficult.

His happy mood fled forever upon reaching the arena parking lot.

Three men approached in different directions — one facing him, the others from opposite sides. Robb's eyes narrowed when he noticed distinctive skull caps adorning their heads with the same distinctive symbol emblazoned on each cap.

A crown of thorns tinged in blood.

His heart pounded, vibrating like a struck tuning fork. Why were agents from the Order of the Crimson Thorns here? What did they want from him? Robb swallowed hard and took a calming breath.

Showing fear was the worst thing to do right now.

"I made it clear I was done." His brown eyes hardened as he met the gaze of the lead agent facing him. "I don't like repeating myself."

The lead agent planted himself in front of Robb and crossed his arms. He gave a brief nod to his fellow agents. Both stopped mere inches from Geoff and Robb.

"You don't dictate to The Order what happens," the lead agent said. "You chose to be one of us."

"I made that choice at one time — out of desperation," Robb said. "But so much has changed since then. My life has changed. I'll tell you the same thing I told Mark earlier. I … am … retired."

He placed an extra emphasis on the last three words to hammer his point home. The lead agent scowled. Geoff quickly shot his brother a puzzled look.

"Do you know these people? Who are they?"

The lead agent snapped his fingers. A pair of hands seized Robb's arms and twisted them behind his back. Geoff let out a pained shout as another agent did the same to him.

"I did not invite you to be a part of this conversation." The lead agent's dark brown eyes slid over to Geoff. "Be silent or I'll rip out your tongue with my fingers."

Both eyes emitted a distinct yellow glow. Panic filled every square inch of Geoff's face as he turned and glanced at Robb, silently pleading for help.

"Look, all I want in life is to be a teacher." Robb spoke in measured tones, trying to suppress rising anger and fear mingling inside him. "I'm thankful for what The Order did for me, but I paid my debt."

What more did they want from him?

He fulfilled his end of the deal they struck to make his student loan debt vanish. Robb performed his required service. Now things were different. He and Amy had a spring wedding a year earlier. They were ready to start a new chapter in their lives together.

One not involving the Order of the Crimson Thorns.

"Your refusal to adhere to the council's wishes cannot go unpunished," the lead agent said.

He gestured toward the agent restraining Geoff. The other man whispered into his brother's right ear. Geoff scrunched up his face like his nostrils caught the aroma of rancid mayonnaise.

His lips started to tremble.

Trembling turned to ear-piercing screams.

"Something is burrowing through my head!" Geoff clenched his teeth and unleashed desperate violent groans. "Help me! I think I'm gonna die!"

The agent restraining him released his arms and let Robb's brother sink to the ground. Geoff clutched both sides of his skull. His screams climbed higher in pitch and louder in volume.

Blood trickled out from both nostrils.

Robb cast his eyes frantically around the parking lot, searching for help. Dull beams from a nearby light pole revealed no people approaching other vehicles near their parking spot. Nobody was around with the power to stop the horror unfolding before him.

"The council decides when your debt is paid," the lead agent said. "No one else."

He drew a pistol and shoved the barrel inside Geoff's open mouth. A sudden explosion of blood, bone, and brain tissue snapped Robb's mind back to the motel room. Tears dribbled down both cheeks. He brushed them away with his fingertips.

His internet search turned up a list of supernatural nexuses. Places housing the right proportions of mystical energy to allow Robb to mask his aura from detection while he used the amulet to build his power. Standing against the Order and destroying every council member in the same manner their agents destroyed Geoff required becoming a powerful being in every sense.

One supernatural nexus caught his eye. A small Colorado town near the Rocky Mountains. Robb counted this discovery as a stroke of good fortune. He could easily blend into this place and disappear until the appointed time to enact his revenge arrived.

Deer Falls would serve as his new refuge.

5

Robb almost laughed out loud when he first laid eyes on the town sign next to the highway shoulder. Two log posts held a flat rectangular sign with a curved top. The sign, suspended between each post, featured bold white lettering beneath an image of a mule deer inside a circle.

Welcome to Deer Falls. Heart of the Rockies.

Heart of the Rocky Mountains?

A claim equal parts quaint and arrogant.

Still, Robb wished he arrived here sooner. His trip to Deer Falls had been delayed while he did everything in his power to throw agents from The Order off his scent. Robb used temporary masking spells to hide his presence and then journeyed town to town throughout Colorado planting false leads concerning his true destination. He only headed to Deer Falls once he grew convinced that he deceived the agents enough to buy himself a little peace.

Robb crossed over a bridge covering a creek flowing along the western edge of Deer Falls. A pale green sign with white lettering identified it as Bobcat Creek. He drove a half-mile beyond the bridge, passing a smattering of houses and businesses flanking the highway before pulling into a corner convenience store.

Two priorities topped Robb's to-do list beyond refilling his gas tank:

finding a low-key job and renting a secure apartment. Following this plan promised to keep him off one specific radar in this one-horse town. Growing strong enough to stand against the Order of the Crimson Thorns mandated extra time and preparation. Agents prematurely uncovering his hiding spot was the last thing Robb needed or desired.

Robb bought a copy of the *Deer Falls Bulletin* inside the convenience store and brought it back to his sedan. Typical small-town weekly newspaper. Boring articles chronicling mundane community events. Not much else. He flipped to classified ads filling a back page and scanned through job listings.

One posting instantly caught his eye.

"Assistant Principal — Deer Falls High School."

Robb cracked a knowing smile after reading the job title aloud. Fate brought him to this place.

He ran across the same posting on a job site while doing an internet search before checking out of his last motel room. The listing was dated 30 days earlier, so Robb assumed the position had already been filled. This more recent posting told him a different story. A welcome change from his original assumptions.

Working as an assistant principal at a small-town high school fit well with his broader plans.

Robb folded up the newspaper again and tossed it aside on the passenger seat before driving away from the convenience store. He scoured Deer Falls for a place to spend the night before settling on a bed-and-breakfast in a Victorian house at the north end of town.

A single car was parked in front, near the sign, when Robb stopped there. He admired the condition of the house. New windows with white trim and restored tawny bricks made the place appear as though it had been built only a year ago instead of a century earlier. His eyes trailed from side to side as he ambled along a stone path and past twin stone pillars up to the front door.

A tiny bell jangled when Robb cracked open the door. The sound stirred a gray-haired woman seated behind a small desk. She set down a pencil and a book of crossword puzzles and glanced up at her visitor.

"Do you have a reservation?"

"I'm afraid not."

"Are you looking for a room?"

Hope mirroring her inquiry filled her eyes as she met Robb's gaze. He smiled and nodded.

"If you have one to spare, I'd be grateful." Robb turned his head and studied a long straight staircase. "First day in town. I haven't settled into a new place yet."

"You are in luck." Her voice bubbled with excitement. "We usually get more foot traffic on weekends. Middle of the week is much quieter."

His eyes trailed away from the staircase and settled on the gray-haired bed-and-breakfast owner again.

"I don't mind quiet," Robb said. "A quiet place is exactly what I need at the moment."

"The room is $146 per night," she said. "We include free 5G wi-fi and streaming. And I prepare a made-from-scratch breakfast every morning during your stay."

"I'm sold."

Her smile deepened when Robb dug out his wallet and passed her a credit card. Paying with his smartphone would be more convenient but agents from The Order would need more time to crack through a phony card to find him. The owner's fingers danced across a keyboard as she entered his information into her computer. She handed Robb's card back to him a couple of minutes later, along with a room key card.

Robb gathered his tote bags and duffell bags from his sedan and returned inside. He climbed the carpeted stairs and headed straight for a bedroom at the end of the hall. Doors leading to other second floor bedrooms were all closed. Flowery wallpaper covered the walls from one end of the hall to the other. Robb dropped his bags on the floor and fished his room key card out of his pocket. He let the door lock behind him again after moving his belongings inside the room.

Cramped took on a whole new meaning within this bedroom. Robb never suffered from claustrophobia. Staying inside this room longer than necessary might change that fact. How did they squeeze a queen-sized bed through the narrow doorway? Between the bed, a dresser, and a nightstand, scant floor space remained bare.

Robb dropped his bags on the bed and unplugged the lamp atop the nightstand. He set the lamp on the floor and pulled the nightstand forward, creating a makeshift desk. No email notifications popped up when he flipped open the laptop and cleared out the screen saver.

He clicked on his email inbox and stared at the last message Amy sent him. The subject line lingered on the laptop screen like an eyesore.

HAPPY THOUGHTS!

Robb gnawed on his lower lip as he opened the email yet again. Smiling face emojis and Kiss-blowing emojis peppered the message. He lost track of how many times he read her words while trying to make sense of what led to Amy's betrayal. They were supposed to be soulmates. She repeated this sentiment often, and he devoured each word with an insatiable hunger. Nobody ended up being a bigger fool than him for believing such nonsense.

Amy spared no effort to make him feel that way. Their last moment together lingered fresh in his mind. It ended with her trying to split his skull open with an ax.

"You just can't leave well enough alone, can you?" she shouted. "Our lives were arranged perfectly for us. You had to ruin everything!"

Her cheeks bore a deepening shade of crimson. Amy drew heavy breaths while standing behind an overturned futon. Sweat drenched her tank top. A lump formed in Robb's throat as he backed away from a shattered lamp.

"I thought you understood," he said. "We're supposed to be on the same side."

Darkness consumed her green eyes like a blackened flame. The same shadowy hue spread over her brown curls down to the tips.

"We will never be on the same side again."

A guttural tone overtook Amy's voice as she spoke those words. Robb bit down on his lower lip. Now he finally understood why Amy attacked him with such fury. She had surrendered herself to become a vessel for The Order to use at their discretion. Now Amy housed a formerly disembodied acolyte.

Only a shell remained of the wife he knew.

"I can't stay here with you," he said. "You've made that impossible for me."

Robb opened his palm and scattered a thin line of salt between himself and the futon. He uttered a brief incantation. Amy shrieked and flung the ax at the front door. It spiraled toward Robb but stopped in mid-air and dropped to the carpet as though the ax struck an invisible wall.

Once he ran out the door, Robb kept running without glancing back. Shoving Amy out of his mind since that day was not an easy or simple task. Robb contemplated deleting the email that had triggered the unwelcome flashback more than once. He dared not follow through with that action. Deletion only equaled waving a white flag and admitting defeat.

Gaining power through the reaper amulet offered them a second chance at building a life together. Robb would restore Amy to her former self soon enough. Once he destroyed the ruling council, she would join him at his side once again.

Robb closed the email and cast his brown eyes at the unzipped tote bag. The reaper amulet's silver chain poked out from underneath a neatly folded pair of dress socks. He pushed the socks aside and snatched up the amulet.

"I need to learn how this works," he mumbled.

His eyes slid back to the door, instinctively checking the knob and deadbolt to see if both were still locked. Robb didn't expect visitors. He took tons of precautions to cover his tracks from using fake credit cards to logging into secure VPN networks. Still, agents from The Order had a nasty habit of turning up in unexpected places at the wrong times.

Satisfied he was alone, Robb's eyes settled back on the amulet. He opened a fresh incognito browser window on his laptop and entered an encrypted database.

The database functioned as a digital repository of ancient knowledge. Since the days of Pax Romana at the height of the Roman Empire, scholars employed by The Order gathered every scrap of information found in every field of study. Every modern library, archive, and search engine paled in comparison to secrets known by The Order and at the fingertips of its agents.

Endless knowledge gathered for one grand purpose.

Infusing the Order of the Crimson Thorns with greater power built upon the darkest magic.

Robb retrieved a webpage bearing a meticulous charcoal drawing of the reaper amulet. The text imparted an impressive promise. Whoever possessed this ancient talisman opened a door to seize the mantle of the Crimson Reaper.

"Is becoming the Crimson Reaper the answer?"

Robb gave voice to a persistent question kicking around inside his head while staring at his laptop screen. It needed to be the answer. He found no better alternative to combat enemies who stole his brother's life and his wife's soul.

A persistent hum from the laptop's internal fan greeted Robb's ears when he clicked on a mystical guide housing instructions for unlocking the reaper amulet's powers. His face fell as he pored over the words splashed across the screen.

Choosing this path demanded a heavy toll.

Drawing on the full magic existing within the amulet required absorbing life energy from seven individual humans. The text described it as their power. Absorbing their power also granted him their individual strengths according to the guide. This energy could only be drawn right as a person crossed the dark threshold separating the living from the dead. One action alone guaranteed the timing would work in his favor.

Robb must slay all seven people himself.

He pinched his lips together while mulling over what the guide demanded. Could he bring himself to slay seven innocent people just to execute this plan? Robb rubbed his hands over his eyes and down his cheeks.

How do I decide who lives and who dies?

Answering that question gnawed at him. He stared at the amulet again. If only The Order and its agents simply left him alone. None of this hiding and scheming would be necessary. Robb only wanted a happy normal life.

A life they denied him.

Robb vowed to return the favor soon enough. Shedding the blood of so many total strangers felt a little unsettling. Then again, did they have a greater right to be alive than Geoff? Why should his brother be the one to get cut down in the prime of his life? That outcome was never fair or right. Robb's actions simply balanced the cosmic scales. If seven random people were compelled to make sacrifices so he could bring down the Order's rulers, then so be it.

One important step lay ahead before Robb now. A rite must be performed to open the amulet as a conduit for absorbing life energy from his intended victims. The guide specified 3:00 am as the exact moment when the rite must be done.

Robb left the bed and breakfast to gather necessary materials for the rite from a local store. Waiting for the designated hour to arrive vexed him. He found himself continually checking the clock on his smartphone's home screen while munching on slices of Italian sausage pizza from Pizza Wagon.

His eyes grew heavier as Robb pored over details of the rite until both eyelids snapped shut.

A persistent tinny ringing greeted his ears. Robb pinched his closed eyelids tighter and scrunched up his face. God, he hated that sound. He released a weary sigh and finally cracked open his eyes.

Robb found himself lying on his side on top of the blankets covering his bed. His eyes trailed over to his smartphone. He snatched the phone off the nightstand and shut off the alarm. Then, he glanced at the time.

2:55 am.

"Son of a bitch! I overslept."

Robb bolted upright. The alarm was supposed to wake him ten minutes earlier.

He scrambled off the bed and prepared for the rite. After drawing back curtains on the nearest window, Robb coated the amulet with ground sage. He slipped the chain over his neck and stood before the window. When his smartphone read 3:00 am, Robb's eyes climbed skyward. The moment had arrived to invoke the incantation and unlock a direct door to the dark ancient magic he sought.

Bright eternal moonlight.

Embrace this amulet.

Release its hidden power.

Protect my flesh.

Infuse my soul.

Let its ancient magic.

Make a new home.

The amulet rested in his open palm while Robb recited the incantation. When he finished, he extended his arm toward the window as far as the chain allowed. A full moon peeked out from behind ashen clouds. Lunar beams bathed each sapphire. A silvery glow enveloped his hand and spread up through Robb's arm. It soon washed over his body from head to toe.

He stood unmoving before the uncovered window until the glowing moonlight absorbed into his skin. Robb let out a relieved sigh and turned back to the laptop. Now the amulet promised him complete protection while he completed his plan.

Robb let the amulet drop to his chest. An anxious energy permeated his whole body as the desire to fall back asleep fled. No worries. Even at this late hour, he could work on the next part of his plan.

Robb cracked open his laptop and went to work polishing up his resume and filling out an application for the assistant principal's job.

6

Eric clenched his teeth and kicked the back rim. He cursed his bad luck. Once his car started wobbling and wildly pulling to the right, he knew he was in deep trouble. His suspicions were confirmed after he pulled the car off the road and rolled to a stop alongside a curb.

A flat tire.

Why here?

Why now?

He was already running late for school this morning. Changing a tire guaranteed Eric wouldn't make it to his first class before the tardy bell rang. An impending trip to the principal's office awaited him. Another clueless lecture from that stupid principal would be his reward.

Eric popped the trunk, pulled out the jack and elevated the rear axle. He fished a lug wrench from the trunk and went to work on the rear passenger side tire. His right hand slipped twice while spinning the wrench, complicating his effort to loosen every lug nut as fast as possible. He let out an angry sigh and blew on his hands. Visible wisps of his breath skirted across his knuckles.

Once Eric spun off the last lug nut, he popped the tire off the hub and rolled it away. Eric rested the flat tire against the curb and hoisted the spare out of the trunk. He mounted the tire and tightened lug nuts again at a pace fit for an audition with a pit crew.

Eric lowered the jack and tossed it, the lug wrench, and the flat tire back inside the trunk. He slammed down the lid and checked his smartphone.

8:11 am.

Dammit. One minute past the second bell.

Deer Falls High was still a mile and a half away from him. Eric jumped in the driver's seat, slammed the door, and turned the key. His car peeled away from the curb and zipped up Center Street toward the high school.

She's waiting at the entrance for me. I know it.

Eric wanted to dismiss that unwelcome thought as simple paranoia. His past experiences with Principal Reynolds told him a different story. She had it in for him since the start of his freshman year. Eric lost count of how many times his mom contemplated turning to home schooling after engaging in a heated argument with that woman. Private schools were too far away from Deer Falls to offer a realistic alternative to the local high school.

He kept his head on a swivel after parking in the senior lot and grabbed his backpack from the passenger seat. Eric's eyes darted from side to side while he sprinted past trees bearing only remnants of a formerly thick kaleidoscope of colorful leaves. He searched for signs of spies who might snitch on him to earn brownie points. Eric slowed his pace to a fast walk when he reached a door on the north end of the building. This side entrance lay on the opposite end from the principal's office.

So did Eric's locker.

And the classroom for first period.

No students or teachers populated the hall beyond the entrance. Eric's nerves tightened like guitar strings. Not seeing a straggler or two only made him feel extra conspicuous. He sprinted inside and headed straight for his locker. Eric slid his backpack off his shoulder as he reached the locker and let it drop to the ground.

34...

A series of clicks emanated from the combination lock as Eric's thumb and fingers turned the dial.

28...

"Nice of you to join us, Mr. Olson."

Eric jumped at the sound of an uninvited familiar voice. His fingers slipped off the combination lock. A distinct aroma of cheap perfume greeted his nostrils. He stood frozen in front of his locker, unwilling to make eye contact with Principal Reynolds.

"You know the policy on tardiness," the principal said. "We've gone over it and the other school rules again and again. You should know them by heart at this point."

"I had a flat tire on my way to school." Eric drew in a sharp breath to try and calm his nerves. "It slowed me up getting here. I changed the tire as fast as possible."

"Is that a fact?"

Her voice sharpened as she posed the rhetorical question. Of course, Principal Reynolds didn't believe him. Big surprise.

"Why would I lie about getting a flat tire?"

Eric kept facing his closed locker door, doing his best to keep his tone measured. His mom told him last time that losing his temper and raising his voice to the principal would only do him more harm than good. He smiled after their conversation because Emily didn't apply the same advice to herself in her interactions with Principal Reynolds.

"An excuse is always resting on the tip of your tongue," Principal Reynolds said. "Taking personal responsibility paves the path to personal success."

Ugh.

Ron always claimed Principal Reynolds was a terrible self-help book brought to life. She never passed up an opportunity to prove him right.

Eric wheeled around and finally made eye contact with his nemesis.

"Do you want me to run outside and get the flat tire?" He swept his arm toward the door leading out to the parking lot. "It's still there inside my trunk. I can roll it into your office. Or snap a picture of the punctured spot and text it to you."

Her eyebrows knit together. Principal Reynolds cast a disapproving scowl at him.

"Mr. Olson, could you stop trying to emulate your older brother?" Exasperation dripped from each word. "I never found his defiant attitude charming or endearing and you're doing nothing to change my mind."

Eric fought the urge to unleash an angry sigh and share his true thoughts about her. He turned away again and refocused his gaze on his locker.

"Can I go to my geography class now?"

Silence greeted his question. Eric popped open his locker and stuffed the backpack inside. He unzipped a pocket and pulled out a textbook, pen, and notebook.

"You may go to your class." Principal Reynolds pierced the uneasy silence between them with a barbed tone. "You will also report to detention after school."

"Detention?" Eric slammed the locker door shut and spun around. "You can't do that to me! I have basketball practice after my last class."

"No. You have detention."

"If I show up late, Coach will have my head on —"

"Actions have consequences, Mr. Olson," she said, cutting him off. "Report to the detention room at 3 pm sharp or I promise it will turn into your new home for the rest of the week."

Principal Reynolds turned on her heel and marched back down the hall leading to her office. Eric scowled as he watched her leave. He instinctively balled up a fist but stopped short of slamming his knuckles into the neighboring locker. Punching the locker door would only draw the principal's attention anew and supply her ammunition for a stiffer punishment.

Eric stewed over his impending stint in detention from first period up through lunch. None of his friends offered any helpful advice for his situation.

"I say we get her fired," Devin said before snatching a cheeseburger off his lunch tray and biting into it.

Eric poked aimlessly at a pile of steamed broccoli on his own tray with a fork. He glanced up and shot Devin a puzzled look.

"I'm down with that. Got any ideas?"

"Plant some weed on her," Devin said after swallowing. "Or hide it in her office."

Tatiana shook her head.

"Anyone over 21 in Colorado can legally use marijuana," she said. "Sorry to burst your bubble."

"What if we claim she tried to give it to one of us?" Devin asked.

"Who do you think the cops will believe?" Tatiana replied. "It won't be the brother of a known pothead."

Devin frowned and took another bite from his burger. Eric didn't blame him for feeling upset. When was she going to stop needling him about his brother? Alex had not smoked a joint for almost a year and a half. He had cleaned up his act enough to start taking classes from Front Range Community College earlier in the spring.

"Look at it this way — you only have one year left to deal with Principal Reynolds. Just find a way to stay off her radar."

Eric snapped his head over to Max. His best friend took a swig from a bottle of cola and shrugged.

"You make it sound so easy, Max." Eric glanced in the other direction at the principal's office. It lay straight across the hall from their cafeteria table. "I don't know how I can grind out a whole year of dealing with her nonstop bullshit."

"Sucks to be you, dude." Max set the half-empty cola bottle down on the table again and met his gaze. "I guess I'm lucky she doesn't bother to do anything to me."

Luck had nothing to do with his spotless record. Principal Reynolds feared Max's father. He had good enough lawyers and deep enough pockets to make the principal's life a living hell. Eric envied him in situations like this one.

"Do me a favor and cover for me at practice," Eric said. "I'll sweet talk Miss Berry into letting me leave detention early. Hopefully, I won't turn up too late."

Max leaned back in his chair and nodded.

"I got your back. You know that."

Eric smiled. He never doubted Max's willingness to come through for him. They had been tight practically since his first day in Deer Falls almost six years ago.

Through each period after lunch, Eric's stomach progressively twisted into tighter knots. Miss Berry seemed nice enough as far as teachers go. She always smiled at him and talked in a singsong tone. Still, she was a teacher. Would any teacher side with a student at odds with their principal?

His instincts told him he didn't stand a chance.

Eric trudged toward the detention room after the final bell rang. Other students zipped past either side of him in a blur from his perspective. Eric's attention focused internally on what he would say to Miss Berry. Ideas for clever tactics to sway her over to his side popped into his head. He brushed them away. Eric settled on telling her the truth. No reasonable person would agree with the punishment Principal Reynolds leveled on him earlier.

Miss Berry had a knack for being reasonable.

She sat at a desk stacked with ungraded papers thumbing through a novel when Eric pushed open the classroom door. No other students were in the room except him. His eyes drifted back to Miss Berry's book. Her left hand partially covered the title, but Eric recognized the visible words. His lips formed a brief smile before snapping back into a frown. Miss Berry never told him she was a fan of his mom's stories. Maybe he could promise her a new paperback complete with a personalized autograph inside the front cover in exchange for his freedom.

Miss Berry snapped her head upward when Eric let the door swing shut behind him. A cheerful smile flooded her full lips. She planted a bookmark in the open page and slapped the novel back down on her cluttered desk.

"I didn't expect to see you here again so soon." Miss Berry's smile devolved into a disappointed half-frown. "You need to stop butting heads with the principal."

"It wasn't my fault this time," Eric said. "I promise."

She brushed back a lock of her long dishwater blonde hair and sighed. "What happened?"

"I got a flat tire on the way to school and got here late. The principal thought I was lying."

"She didn't believe you?"

Eric shifted the backpack strap threatening to fall off his shoulder.

"Yeah. I got a raw deal. I even offered to show her the flat in the trunk. Didn't matter. Her mind was made up."

Miss Berry tugged on her glasses resting on her nose and leaned back in her chair. She shook her head.

"She thought you lied about getting a flat tire. Wow."

"Anyway, I was hoping you'd let me out of here early, so I don't miss any practice." Eric cast a quick glance back into the hall before refocusing his gaze on the teacher. "If I show up late, Coach Watkins will bench me before our season opener."

Miss Berry's smile returned.

"I've got you marked down. You're good to go."

Eric matched her happy expression with a bright grin of his own.

"Thank you so much. I owe you big time."

"Yeah, you do. You better help us get a state title this season."

Eric turned and started for the door. He paused in the doorway and gave Miss Berry a sideways glance.

"What will you do if Principal Reynolds finds out I took off from detention early?"

She bit down on her lower lip for a second before releasing it again.

"I'll tell her she needs to add more zeros to the end of my paycheck."

Eric's smile broadened as he turned away a second time and closed the door behind him. It felt good to finally outfox that stupid principal for a change.

7

Robb straightened up against the chair back and adjusted the Windsor knot on his purple striped necktie. The office door shut with a thud and caused a brief rattle in the closed blinds. His eyes slid over to the principal as she walked past his chair with a sheet of paper in her hand. She was an ordinary mousy brunette pushing 50 and dressed in an unflattering beige pantsuit.

"You have an impeccable resume, Mr. Cooper." She gave him an approving nod and set the paper on her desk. "It's so rare for us to get a teacher boasting your qualifications here in Deer Falls, let alone an assistant principal."

Robb leaned forward in his chair.

"My personal motto, Principal Reynolds, is this: be the best version of yourself in everything you do."

Principal Reynolds cracked a smile and took a seat behind the desk. She met his gaze.

"Only students and their parents use that title. Please call me Lora."

He returned her smile with another.

"Sounds good, Lora."

She offered another approving nod and rested her arms on the desk. "That's better."

Her brown eyes drifted back down to the single sheet of paper she carried earlier. Lora cleared her throat and raised the paper to get a closer look.

"I'm encouraged by your personal motto," she said. "Excellence is one thing we demand above everything else at Deer Falls High. We strive to elevate ourselves in academics, athletics, and other facets of student life."

Lora turned and pointed to a bronze plaque mounted on the wall behind her. The principal quickly faced Robb again and droned on about recognition she and others at the school had received for various accomplishments. He gave his wristwatch a side-eye glance. Robb found it harder to keep a smile painted on his lips as she kept babbling. If this job didn't fill a pertinent need, he would gladly tell Lora exactly how stupid and meaningless every accomplishment inspiring her boasts appeared in his eyes. He resisted yielding to those urges.

Playing along with her was a necessary evil — at least for the moment.

"Wouldn't you agree, Robb?"

He paused, unsure of how to respond. Robb cursed himself for letting his mind wander. How would he ever land this job if he didn't listen to every annoying word dribbling out of her annoying face?

"Everything you said is right on the money."

Robb straightened up in his chair and punctuated his statement with a thumbs up. Lora's face beamed with pride at his response. His smile and internal revulsion deepened in equal measure. Being forced to pretend he cared about anything she said made him want to vomit whatever remained of his breakfast bagel.

Still, Robb played the part he needed to play with exactness. He approached every question she posed with syrupy feel-good answers torn from the pages of cookie-cutter inspirational self-help books. Robb did his best to speak what he perceived as being her language. If that's what it took to nail this interview, so be it.

His strategy seemed to be paying off.

"When would you be available to start?" Lora asked, as their interview wound down.

"I'm flexible. I can start as early as Monday."

She glanced down at a desk calendar and smiled.

"I have a couple of more interviews to conduct today, but I'll let you know what we decide within the next 24 to 48 hours."

"Perfect." Robb rose from his chair and extended his hand. "I look forward to hearing from you."

Lora simultaneously rose from her chair and shook his hand. Doubts started to creep into his mind once Robb left the principal's office and walked outside the school to his car. Did he do enough to secure this job? What if other candidates she planned to interview later left a better impression?

"I can't leave anything to chance," Robb muttered. "I need to know what the future holds for certain."

He crossed the street to the visitor's parking lot and unlocked his car door with a clicker. Robb sank down in the driver's seat and whipped out his smartphone. If Deer Falls was truly a supernatural nexus, he should have no trouble tracking down a local psychic or medium to give him a reading.

Robb's voice search for "Deer Falls psychic" yielded a promising result. The search engine directed him to a psychic who worked out of a parlor on the southern end of Deer Falls — about three miles away from the high school. Perfect. If she was as effective as psychics he knew back in Denver, Robb could set his mind fully at ease until he heard back from Lora later. He shut the car door and peeled out of the parking lot.

A swinging ramshackle black sign hung from a six-foot tall pole outside a modest shop connected to a larger ranch house. Two words — psychic reader — adorned the sign in faded neon lettering. Robb parked along a curb outside the house. He loosened his necktie, tossed it aside, and unbuttoned the top button on his dress shirt. The chain holding the reaper amulet peeked out from under the collar.

Robb popped out of the car and walked at a brisk pace up to the shop's front door. A glass window next to the door advertised tarot card readings and palm readings. Each word stood out on the glass in bright bold lettering painted with window markers. Drawn brown curtains obscured the room beyond the window itself.

A small bell clinked atop the door when he pushed it open. On cue, a woman emerged from a back room and parted beads to join Robb inside the shop's main room.

"Welcome fellow traveler," she said. "How can I guide your journey through the mystical realm today?"

She brushed back flowing chestnut locks that fell past her shoulders. The psychic wore a tight colorful blouse and matching skirt that fell to her ankles. Silver hoop earrings dangled from each earlobe.

"I'm here for a reading," he said. "I have a lot on my mind. A few things are unsettled."

"The spirits want to settle your mind, friend." She directed him to a cushioned chair at a round wooden table near the curtained-off window. "They see the path ahead of you and will guide you where you need to go."

An irritated frown crept over Robb's lips. She affected a phony accent that already grated on his nerves. Why couldn't she speak like a normal person? Her accent coupled with her outfit reminded him of a fortune teller from a terrible B movie.

None of the psychics in Denver he was familiar with ever acted like this woman.

"I am Angelique." The psychic stretched out her arms with open palms turned upward and glanced skyward. "I will serve as your conduit with the spiritual realm."

Angelique sat in a second cushioned chair directly across from Robb and met his gaze again. A large crystal ball and a deck of tarot cards sat on the table between them. All cards were stacked in a haphazard pile. She rested her right arm on the table's edge and held the left one out to him.

"Give me your hand."

Robb followed her instruction and offered his right hand. Angelique brought both hands forward. She clasped the underside of his hand and traced the lines in his palm with her index finger.

"Your heart line is in flux," her voice took on a concerned tone. "You recently experienced the loss of someone close to you."

"I did."

"I sense maybe a spouse or a parent."

His eyes widened.

A spouse or a parent?

She was trying to pawn off a random cold read hoping he'd volunteer the necessary information on his own. Angelique was nothing more than an irritating fraud. Robb tore his hand away from her grasp.

"How about we skip to the tarot cards?"

Angelique flashed him a puzzled look. She shrugged a second later and slid the cards closer to her. The psychic shuffled the cards and began laying them down in the center of the table, exposing the face for both her and Robb to see clearly. Each card Angelique drew caused his throat to tighten.

The tower.

Seven of swords.

10 of swords.

The wheel of fortune.

The magician.

Robb leaned over as she laid down each card. Angelique's eyes drifted up to his neck. She paused and visibly gulped. He glanced down at his chest. The reaper amulet peeked out from under the top two unbuttoned buttons. His eyes snapped back up to her.

"I sense great upheaval for you." Angelique quickly shifted her gaze back to the cards. "Betrayal is the incubator of change. Beware of seeking power. It will lead to further betrayal and an untimely end."

Robb narrowed his eyes. Did this would-be psychic just threaten him? Her words sure sounded like coded language spoken by an agent of the Order of the Crimson Thorns hiding in plain sight.

He tugged on a loose thread on a button just below his cuff. Robb held up a finger and drew out a pocketknife from his pants. Angelique froze in her cushioned chair. Her eyes were glued to the pocketknife.

"I hate loose threads." He unfolded a six-inch serrated blade and grabbed the thread. "Always a problem with dress shirts, you know?"

Robb sliced through the thread and gave a satisfied nod. Her shoulders loosened and she let out a slight sigh. He smiled and rose from the chair.

"You know what else I hate?"

Robb seized Angelique's right wrist and slammed it on the table. He drove his serrated blade through flesh and bone, pinning the limb to the wooden top.

"I hate phony psychics."

Angelique shrieked. Pain and terror flooded her voice in equal measure. Blood dribbled out around the wound and pooled on the table under her stationary limb. Robb couldn't help chuckling.

She obviously didn't see that coming.

"Now it's my turn to do a palm reading for you." He circled the table as he spoke. "Judging by your shortened lifeline, I sense a major change headed your way."

Angelique sobbed and tried to grab the knife handle with her other hand. Robb smacked it away.

"The only untimely end will be yours."

Tears and streaks of mascara coursed down her cheeks. Angelique's lips trembled.

"I don't want to die. I'll do anything you want. Please don't kill me."

Sobs choked her voice. Her fake accent from earlier had vanished. Robb walked behind a counter display case showing off an assortment of overpriced healing crystals and runes. He scoured around the cash register for a makeshift weapon. Scissors. A box cutter. Anything to silence the psychic's blubbering.

"You don't have a problem with insinuating my death," Robb said. "Let me tell you. I can't be stopped. Not by you. Not by The Order. Not by anyone."

"The Order? I don't know what you're —"

"Don't play dumb with me. You saw my amulet. You were sent to this one-horse town to trail me."

"I've lived in Deer Falls my whole life. I … I … Oh God, I have a daughter … Please don't kill me."

Robb paused in his search and stared at her. Maybe he miscalculated. Perhaps she wasn't an agent of The Order after all. Just a huckster who picked the wrong person to con.

He glanced down at the chain holding the reaper amulet and smiled. One action would save this from being a colossal waste of his time.

"Fuck it," Robb said. "I'll just improvise."

Robb finally found a box cutter inside a cubby hole underneath the register. Angelique's eyes widened as he marched over toward the table again. Still weeping, she grabbed the pocketknife handle and tried to extract the blade from the table and her wrist. Robb stopped directly behind her. He pressed his hand against Angelique's chin and snapped her head backward.

"I'm afraid this conduit to the spiritual realm is now closed for business," he said.

Robb dragged the box cutter across Angelique's throat. The blade ripped through flesh, leaving a trail of oozing blood in its wake. Angelique gurgled and lurched forward in her chair when he drew his hand away again.

He raised the amulet and pressed the crossed sickle blades against her forehead. A glowing energy flowed from her face into the amulet and up through his hand. Robb gasped as it surged from one end of his body to the other. Such an incredible rush. Unlike anything he had ever experienced — skydiving included.

Her life energy now belonged to him.

Robb felt twice as powerful compared to when he first entered the room. Angelique slumped over in the chair. Her vacant eyes were transfixed on scattered tarot cards.

"Angelique, honey, is everything okay? I heard crying and screaming out here."

Robb wheeled around. A man with a brown goatee stood in an open doorway connecting the shop to the ranch house.

Shit.

Another loose thread.

The goateed man's eyes trailed down to Angelique's body. He screamed and cupped his hand to his mouth. His eyes shifted over to the box cutter hanging loose in Robb's hand.

"You murdered my girlfriend!"

Tears trickled down his cheeks as he shouted those four words at Robb. Angelique's boyfriend turned on his heel and ran back inside the house. Robb sprang forward. He couldn't let that bastard flee and call the police. Those filthy maggots would throw a major wrench into his plans in a hurry.

He needed to buy himself more time.

Robb gave the door a hard shove when her boyfriend turned to slam it shut and barricade it behind him. He stumbled backward and landed hard on the tile floor. Once inside, Robb dove on top of him and slammed the back of his head against the tile. Angelique's boyfriend flailed his arms, trying to force Robb off his chest.

Robb kept beating his head against the floor until her boyfriend stopped moving and blood oozed from both ears. He took the pendant and pressed it against the boyfriend's forehead, mirroring his earlier actions with Angelique. Fresh life energy surged through Robb, adding to the power now inhabiting his frame.

Two down.

Five to go.

8

This didn't stand out as the worst crime scene Sheriff Leeds ever encountered in Deer Falls but easily ranked near the top of the list. The sheer brutality and rage blew him away. A double homicide. One victim died from a severe skull fracture. The other victim suffered a stab wound through her wrist and a slit throat. Both bore peculiar cross-shaped imprints on their foreheads.

Laying eyes on their bloody corpses left him with a queasy feeling in his belly.

"The victims have been identified as Angelique Woods and her boyfriend Troy McCord. Both were long-time residents of Deer Falls. Angelique was a local psychic and fortune teller, while Troy —"

"I know who they are, Deputy Parks." Leeds pivoted and faced his fellow officer. "I know both families well. This is heartbreaking."

Parks nodded.

"Their seven-year-old daughter came home from a playdate with a friend and found her parents deceased," he said. "She ran crying and screaming over to the next-door neighbor's house. That's when we got the call."

"My God. That's horrible."

"I contacted the little girl's grandparents. They came and picked her up shortly before you arrived."

Leeds pressed a hand against his mouth and fought a momentary urge to vomit. He couldn't imagine the sheer grief, terror, and loneliness afflicting that poor child after encountering her parents' dead bodies. She didn't deserve any of this.

"Do we have any leads on a suspect?" he asked.

Parks glanced down at the notepad in his hand.

"Nothing solid yet. I talked to the neighbors. One witness saw a light brown sedan park out front a little after 3 pm and a tall brown-haired man go into the shop."

"Did they give you a license plate number or a detailed description of the man?"

The deputy shrugged.

"No one paid close enough attention to give me anything else useful. The neighbor who saw the man didn't think much about it because customers regularly came over to see Ms. Woods for readings."

Leeds turned and walked from the kitchen back into the reading room. Parks followed on his heels. Angelique's body had been placed inside a body bag and was wheeled out on a stretcher right when they re-entered the psychic's shop. Numbers identifying crime scene evidence dotted the table, the chair, and the surrounding carpet where Angelique had been slain. A crime scene photographer stood parallel to the cushioned chair, snapping photos.

"Did we find a murder weapon?" Leeds asked.

"Not yet," Parks said. "Nothing conclusive turned up from finger-prints either. I hope DNA tests offer some useful leads. Our unsub did a pretty good job of covering their tracks."

Leeds stared at the table. His eyes settled on a spot where blood had pooled around Angelique's wrist. Torn fabric and a puncture mark in the wood from a knife blade lay in the center of the blood-stained portion.

"This unsub made a mistake somewhere," he said. "I feel it in my bones. It's our job to identify their mistake."

An uneasiness settled on Leeds as he left the shop and returned to his cruiser. This already promised to be a complicated murder case. Then again, what else was new? Nothing in Deer Falls ever proved to be simple. While he relished living here, close to the mountains, too many strange and unexplained things regularly happened in this town.

Leeds threw his vehicle into reverse and headed back toward the sheriff's office. His mind drifted back to a conversation with Deputy Palmer during his first year on the job in Deer Falls. What his friend and mentor said at the time stuck with him from day one.

"Always remember one thing," he said. "Deer Falls is a different beast when it comes to law enforcement."

He raised his eyebrows and shot a puzzled look at Palmer. What was he trying to tell him with such a cryptic statement?

"This is a cozy mountain town," Leeds said. "How is it any worse than any other place?"

Leeds took a job as a deputy in Deer Falls specifically because it offered the promise of serving in a peaceful and beautiful community. A safe place where he and Mariah could raise their family together. His wife was already four months pregnant when they packed up and left Albuquerque to start their new life here.

Palmer didn't indulge in the same brand of optimism.

"You're new here, Jackson, but you'll learn soon enough," he said. "Some things happen here that defy explanation. Living in Deer Falls means dealing with more than a human element."

Palmer rose from his desk and walked over to a rolling cork board in the corner of his office. Numerous notes and photos pinned across the board detailed an ongoing kidnapping case. Leeds had given the board's contents a cursory glance when he first walked into the office to chat with Palmer. Now his eyes drifted over and centered on the collected photos and notes.

"Charlie Bowers doesn't return home from school one day." Palmer pointed to a photo of a young boy occupying a prominent spot near the center of the board. "Parents have no idea what happened to him. Kidnappers made demands in exchange for the child's freedom. Classic kidnapping case, right?"

"Yeah, I heard about it on the news a couple of days before Mariah and I moved here."

"What you didn't hear is that, according to his parents, Charlie was stolen from them because of a debt. His father wanted to make a killing in cryptocurrency and struck a deal with a demon to make it happen."

Leeds stared unblinking at his fellow deputy. His mouth dropped open a second later.

"What the hell? Are you serious? That's the biggest bunch of nonsense I've ever —"

Palmer glanced back and shook his head.

"That's just it. I don't think it is nonsense. Strange things happen here. The Bowers family went from living in a crummy rundown trailer to building a mansion out in The Ranches district almost overnight."

"Are we sure he wasn't just running a drug ring?"

"I checked it out. He came back clean on that front. No. Alan Bowers plunged headfirst into crypto trading."

Leeds rubbed his chin as he stared at the missing boy's photo. It seemed infinitely more plausible that rival cryptocurrency traders were behind this kidnapping than a pact with the devil.

"Alan claims the demon showed up demanding a cut of the profits." Palmer turned and met his gaze. "When he balked, the demon summoned a minion to snatch Charlie at the school bus stop."

Leeds scoffed and shook his head.

"That's ridiculous. Sounds like the dad did something to his kid if you ask me."

"He's basically doing it right now. Alan confessed the demon will only return Charlie if he immediately surrenders his body, soul, and wealth for not honoring the earlier deal."

"Let me guess. The dad is hung up on the wealth part of the equation."

"Bingo."

Leeds turned away and gazed outside the office window. His eyes settled on one of their dispatchers sitting at her desk wearing headphones, taking a call.

"If we assume what he's saying is true, and there really are demons out there doing these things, then why don't we do something about it?" Leeds asked. "Why keep it quiet? Shouldn't we warn the public?"

Silence met his questions. Leeds wheeled around to face Palmer again. He crossed his arms and frowned at the younger deputy.

"We can't ever let this sort of information become public knowledge," Palmer said. "Putting the word out that Deer Falls is an active breeding ground for monsters, witches, demons, and other supernatural creatures would cripple our town economically and send everyone into a justifiable panic. It would destroy more lives than these creatures could ever destroy by themselves."

"Then what do we do?"

"We keep everything close to the vest. Solve cases? Yes. Bring criminals to justice? Definitely. But it's also our job to create cover stories and let people believe the world they see on cable news every day is the actual world we live in."

Leeds felt the sting of those instructions when Palmer met his demise only a few years later. It pained him to conceal what truly happened to his mentor in the interest of safeguarding against a public meltdown.

Witnessing the brutality of these new murders evoked comparisons to Palmer's corpse. Finding him pinned against the wall of the decrepit Graber house still haunted Leeds during quiet moments when he pondered his old friend's fate. Bullet holes riddled his upper body. A sharpened walking stick punctured his navel, impaling Palmer like a chunk of meat on a kabob.

An ancient witch murdered Deputy Palmer — along with several other Deer Falls residents — before a group of kids vanquished her and trapped the malevolent being inside a locked chest. Fear flooded Leeds' mind after his thoughts traveled back to the present. What if another witch or a similarly powerful being had a hand in causing these latest deaths?

Leeds wanted to discount a supernatural element. Still, he couldn't ignore that strange symbol burned into the foreheads of both bodies. It resembled a cross in some ways, but also bore characteristics unlike any other cross he had ever seen.

What did it all mean?

Who or what butchered that poor couple?

Leeds turned into the parking lot behind the sheriff's office and parked his cruiser near the rear entrance. He called Mariah to let her know he'd be working late again. She promised to put a plate of pot roast and potatoes in the fridge for him to reheat when he came home. Dinner had to wait. Leeds hated to cut into family time, but he also couldn't rest until he gave himself and his deputies firmer evidence to go on in this case.

He ducked into the station and headed straight to his office. Leeds cracked open his laptop and retrieved the crime scene photos their photographer had loaded into the department database. Seeing their lifeless bodies from different angles sent another quick shudder down his spine.

Leeds clicked on the zoom button and enlarged one photo for a closer look at the strange forehead symbol that caught his eye earlier. It took the shape of a traditional cross. Each bar resembled a sickle blade, however, instead of a beam.

An unfamiliar design.

Searching for information on a regular search engine turned up nothing helpful. Leeds let out a reluctant sigh. He knew one place where he could obtain the information he sought — despite how much he loathed going down that specific rabbit hole. He frowned and opened a browser window housing a portal to a dark web connected search engine.

Leeds typed "sickle blade cross" into the search bar. Page one of the search results turned up numerous odd images. None of the imagery quite fit the dimensions and pattern of the symbol at the crime scene. Later pages in the results were increasingly less helpful.

"This will take me forever," he mumbled. "I got to approach this from a different direction."

Leeds pulled up a dark web message board. Criminals routinely connected with one another through the board to arrange off-the-books transactions. It also offered an ideal virtual gathering place for the seedier supernatural element to make connections.

Yo fam. Jay-El here. Can anyone hook me up with a sickle blade cross?

Three dots flashed below his message, indicating someone typing a response.

Sickle blade cross? WTF?

Never heard of it, bruh.

U makin shit up?

Leeds frowned and rubbed his chin. He only saw the symbol for the first time less than an hour ago. How in the hell was he supposed to know its actual name? He made a copy of the crime scene photo and cropped out the part of the forehead showing the symbol. Leeds attached the new photo file in a new message.

More dots appeared below the message.

I know that symbol. The reaper amulet.

Reaper amulet? Leeds scratched his head. Why did their unsub burn this symbol on the foreheads of his victims? He needed more information.

Reaper amulet? What's that?

8

Leeds leaned back in his chair. No new message came through below his question. He sighed after waiting a couple of minutes and retyped the question.

This time, the moving dots reappeared.

Stay away from it, dawg.

Deep magic. Will mess U up.

Taking this anonymous message board user's advice wasn't a feasible option. This amulet offered a ticket to cracking this case open. Still, this new information confirmed a lingering fear Leeds didn't want confirmed.

Either an occult-influenced killer or a supernatural entity had perpetrated the double homicide.

$$9$$

Eric ran the same drill dozens of times in other practices. Every cut, screen, and pass soaked into his muscle memory from so much repetition. Or so he thought. After goofing up the same cut twice in a row, doubts crept into his head.

Coach Watkins' temper seeped out at an equal rate.

"Pay attention, Olson!" he snapped. "You're cutting too close to the screener. If you don't allow enough space for a drive and kick, the defender will force a tough shot or a steal and suddenly we give up an easy transition basket on the other end."

Eric pinched his lips together and nodded. He resisted the urge to tell Coach Watkins what he thought about his playbook. Their team emphasized playing the pass so much that it complicated far too many offensive possessions. This style of play offered a sure formula for sucking fun out of basketball.

All those thoughts stayed in his head where they belonged. Eric already found himself fighting to keep his spot in the starting lineup. He didn't need to provide extra fuel to make benching him an easier decision for Coach Watkins.

"Let's get it right this time," Coach Watkins said. "Run the high pick and roll again."

He blew his whistle to set the play in motion.

Eric made a cut to the opposite wing, this time leaving enough space for the screener near the top of the key. Trace, their point guard, drove past the screen and attacked the rim. His defender bit on a fake kick out to Eric in the corner and Trace scored an easy layup. Coach Watkins blew his whistle again after the basket and gave both players a brief approving nod.

"Much better," he said. "Make the proper cuts and create enough space, then good things will happen."

Finally getting the play right helped Eric settle into a better rhythm as practice progressed. He executed the team's down screen and triple box plays exactly how they were drawn up in the playbook. Then, Eric forced back-to-back turnovers during defensive drills.

Only one thing left to conquer before practice ended.

Free throws.

Eric gnawed on his lower lip as Coach Watkins told all the players to gather around him at the top of the key while he doled out a handful of final instructions. For whatever reason, his coach delighted in putting Eric on the spot at the end of practice. Make two free throws and everyone heads to the locker room. Miss one or both and everyone finishes the day with extra sprints first.

Every second felt like it lasted 10 minutes.

"Bring it in," Coach Watkins said.

He raised his fist. Every player placed a hand on top of it while forming a circle around their coach.

"Bucks on three," he said. "One, two, three, Bucks!"

All the players shouted "Bucks!" in unison and they broke the circle. Coach Watkins immediately pointed to Eric and motioned him to the free throw line.

"If Olson makes a free throw," he said. "We're done."

Eric's throat tightened as he stepped to the line amid encouraging cheers from teammates gathered behind him. He drew a deep breath and glanced at the rim. Eric spun the ball in his hand, dribbled twice, and let it fly.

The ball clanked off the front iron.

"You guys know what to do," Coach Watkins said. "Line up behind the baseline."

Eric took his position and raced for the opposite baseline as soon as the whistle blew. He reached down and touched the baseline with his fingertips then turned and sprinted back to the other baseline where he repeated the same motion. Coach Watkins forced the entire roster to do 10 total runs before he finally blew the whistle to officially end practice.

Trace scowled at Eric as he entered the locker room. This wasn't the first time his missed free throws led to extra end-of-practice sprints.

"Don't choke at the line on Friday," he said. "I'd like to win our season opener."

Eric sighed and headed straight to his locker. He cracked open the door and pulled out a towel.

"Worry about making your own shots first," Eric said, glancing back at Trace. "Then you'll earn the right to throw some shade my way."

His teammate flipped him off as he walked away to take a shower. Eric said nothing else, but a few choice words still rested on his tongue. Yeah, he struggled with free throws from time to time. So what? Trace never played a hint of defense and was an erratic shooter. He sure wasn't the second coming of Kobe Bryant or Stephen Curry like he believed and wanted everyone else to believe.

Eric met up with his friends outside the gym after showering and throwing on a long-sleeved baseball shirt, dark blue jeans, and suede jacket. Max glanced over when the gym door closed behind Eric.

"Did you see the latest?" he asked.

Eric flashed a puzzled look at his best friend.

"The latest on what?"

9

"New details on those murders."

Devin glanced up from his smartphone. He showed him the screen.

"People are claiming it was a drug deal gone bad," Devin continued. "They're talking about it all over cable news and YouTube."

"A drug deal?" Eric repeated. "Based on what?"

He always greeted anything cable news reported with skepticism. Much of it had to do with things his mom told him. She always complained that the news networks distorted facts to push a preconceived agenda because a few mega corporations owned every media outlet.

"They didn't really say," Devin said. "It's all a little sus if you ask me."

"Why?" Tatiana looked up from her phone screen. Her brows knitted together while a half-frown hung on her lips. "What's your theory?"

"I texted Alex about it," he replied. "He thinks it was a botched robbery. That sounds about right to me."

Eric snatched Devin's phone out of his hand and stared at the comments below the YouTube video. Most comments shared the usual thoughts and prayers for the orphaned child. A few others spouted conspiracy theories about who committed the crime. He clicked the play button as their group walked from the gym to a set of double doors leading out to the parking lot. The news report shared grim details on the slayings of Angelique Woods and Troy McCord. The sheer brutality of their deaths haunted Eric. He hadn't seen anything like it in Deer Falls since Cassandra roamed free.

Cassandra.

Oh God. Did she commit these murders?

Eric wanted to scrub away that thought as soon as it entered his mind, but it lingered like a permanent stain.

Christina assured him repeatedly she placed a spell on the chest to prevent anyone from unburying it a third time. Eric struggled to convince himself things were so simple. If another powerful witch came along, they could easily break the spell and start the nightmares all over again. And if that happened, who could stop them from bringing back Cassandra for their own purposes?

"What if those murders weren't because of a drug deal or a robbery?"

Voicing his question earned Eric an immediate suspicious look from Tatiana. He passed the phone back to Devin. Max's eyes widened when he connected the dots on what Eric left unspoken. A worried frown washed over his face.

"No." He vehemently shook his head. "It can't be her. You're wrong."

'It feels familiar."

"Dude, we beat her! Don't get shook over this or get me shook either."

Tatiana rolled her eyes and sighed.

"I don't think that crazy gang-banger chick has anything to do with this," she said. "If you start trying to connect her to random murders, you'll never give yourself a chance to heal."

Eric snapped his head at her.

"Cassandra wasn't part of a gang," he said. "She's a witch — a goddamn real-life witch who nearly murdered me and my family."

Tatiana raised her hands in a defensive manner.

"I'm not trying to discredit your trauma," she said. "A violent criminal attacked your family. That's legit terrifying. But she also was an ordinary person, just like me or you."

"Say what?" Anger threaded through Max's voice as he jumped to Eric's defense. "We're not capping. This isn't a big lie. I saw that witch dissolve and get sucked into the chest with my own two eyes."

"You don't know what you saw," Tatiana said. "The police found a gas leak in the house. Gas can cause hallucinations even with short-term exposure. The sheriff's office claimed they found you all tied up in an upstairs bedroom after Cassandra fled town."

"That's a bullshit cover story," Max replied.

Tatiana's lips hardened into a deep frown.

"It's much more plausible than claiming an evil witch killed a bunch of people using dark magic until another witch stopped her," she said.

Eric bit down on his lower lip. The urge to chew out Tatiana lingered in his belly. Once again, she insisted on downplaying their experiences, and force fed him and Max the same cover story everyone else in town already bought. It came off as a not-so-subtle way of insinuating they both lost their minds.

Eric didn't like her implication one bit.

"If she 'fled town" like you said, where has Cassandra been for the last six years?" He chose his words carefully while curling fingers into air quotes. "Why abandon her alleged hostages and not return to finish them off later?"

Tatiana shrugged. She walked a half-step ahead of the others and pushed open one of the twin exit doors.

"I wish I had solid answers for you," she said, not bothering to glance back. "My guess is this girl is on the run and doesn't want to be arrested for being a cop killer. She's probably living somewhere else under a new name and identity."

Eric scowled.

Tatiana had everything already figured out in her head. She blinded her eyes to the truth as much as everyone else in Deer Falls. Still, their collective skepticism didn't sting nearly as much as hers. They had been friends since freshman year. Eric wished she placed more faith and trust in what he and Max said by now.

When Tatiana finally made eye contact with him again, signs of her smug determination to be right melted off her face. She stopped at the front bumper of her car and waited for Eric to catch up to her.

"Are you still suffering from hallucinations?"

He licked his lips.

"Not since we went mountain biking on the Bobcat Creek Trail two months ago. And that was the first one I suffered in a while. Hope it will be the last one too."

A brief smile fluttered onto Tatiana's face. She fiddled with the strap on her handbag.

"I'm happy to hear you're doing better," she said. "I know that was a tough time in your life. The last thing I want is for you to be forced to relive it."

That's the last experience Eric wanted as well. Still, he worried the universe wouldn't offer him a choice in determining his own fate.

10

An energetic smile lingered on Emily's lips after the phone call ended. Logan proved to be a miracle worker. They still needed to hash out a few details on the contract, but her novel, *The Witching Hour*, stood on the verge of being adapted into a Netflix series. He was one hell of an agent. One of Emily's primary goals as a novelist was coming true right before her eyes.

She sank back into her office chair. Emily stared at her latest work-in-progress populating her laptop screen with a satisfied smile. Writing *The Witching Hour* offered a form of therapy for what she experienced while living in Deer Falls. A fictionalized version of those terrifying events offered the only real avenue for sending her story out into the world. Sheriff Leeds — still a deputy at the time — made it clear any efforts to reveal Cassandra's true nature to the media invited unwelcome repercussions for Emily and her sons.

She didn't take well to being threatened. Emily found her muse in defying local authorities and basing her novel around that ancient witch's rampage. It gave her no small amount of satisfaction to see the same story achieve bestseller status. None of the community leaders in Deer Falls dared do anything to suppress the novel — assuming they ever had an ability to do so anyway. Their actions would only force their hand into revealing all the town's dirty supernatural secrets to the outside world.

An impending streaming deal called for a celebration.

"Mom?"

Emily's ears perked up at the sound of Eric's voice. She bounced out of her chair and flung open the door to her office.

"Guess what? I have the best news." Excitement bubbled up in her voice. "You're going to be so thrilled."

Her son turned and met her gaze after closing the front door and locking both deadbolts. His hand clutched a backpack strap resting on his shoulder.

"What's up?"

"I just found out from my agent that Netflix wants to turn *The Witching Hour* into a new series!"

"That's so dope. I'm happy for you, Mom."

Eric offered his fist for a fist bump. Emily experienced a momentary urge to tease him about going all-in on popular teen slang, but she refrained. He'd have ample room for a comeback if he heard her trot out sayings like "gag me with a spoon" from back in the day. She simply bumped fists with her baby boy. Eric smiled and pulled her in for a follow-up hug.

"We need to celebrate," Emily said, drawing back again. "I'm thinking of ordering a large mountain pizza from Pizza Wagon. Wild and crazy. I know."

Eric scrunched up his face and shook his head.

"I'm not in a pizza mood. How about burgers?"

"Burgers are fine — just not the Polar Shack. Their wild west burger was a crime against food."

Emily cringed thinking back to that sorry and soggy excuse for a burger. Both lettuce and tomato tasted like they were left under a heat lamp for a full 24 hours before meeting her lips.

"I heard The Backyard Grille started making a bunch of new burgers different from their old ones. Max told me their new owner changed chefs last month."

"I like the sound of different."

Living in Deer Falls meant limited dining options. Once Emily and her boys cycled through the handful of restaurants and fast-food joints in town during their first year living here, dining out turned boring after a while. Her outlook only changed whenever she returned to Denver to do book signings or traveled outside of Colorado for other author events.

"Go ahead and drop your backpack upstairs," Emily said. "Your homework can wait."

"Cool," Eric said. "Let's jet."

Emily ducked into her office and grabbed her purse. She'd rather celebrate this moment with no one else besides her baby boy.

* * *

Only two other customers were dining inside the burger joint when Emily walked inside. Eric wasn't kidding when he said everyone else in town liked the Polar Shack better. She shook her head at the thought. These people needed to leave Deer Falls more often and sample higher quality food. Sure, The Backyard Grille tasted a little pedestrian, but it still ran circles around the other place.

"Welcome home to The Backyard Grille. May I take your order?"

A freckled teen girl wearing black-rimmed glasses stood behind the counter and flashed an earnest smile. Emily glanced over her shoulder. Eric hung back a few steps with his face buried in his smartphone. His thumbs tapped the screen furiously as he fired off a text.

"What do you want, sweetie?"

He glanced up from the screen. Eric's eyes drifted over to the girl taking their order. He instantly shifted his gaze away from her. A slight shade of crimson appeared in his cheeks.

"Mom …"

Emily flashed a puzzled look at her son. Was he embarrassed to be seen hanging out in public with his mother? A crooked smile soon formed on her lips. Did he like the girl taking their order?

"What burger do you want?" Emily asked, repeating her earlier question.

Eric gazed up at a long rectangular board hanging above the counter. It featured the complete menu, etched across the wood using a pen from a wood burning kit. Clever way to do a menu. Emily gave The Backyard Grille points for being creative with their design.

"I'll get a rancher's choice burger," he said.

Her son kept his face glued to the board. Emily's smile broadened. Eric did everything in his power to avoid making eye contact with the freckle-faced girl.

"I think I want a bacon cheeseburger," she said. "Can I swap mayo for barbecue sauce?"

The freckle-faced girl nodded and punched buttons at the register.

"Do you want a side of house fries and drinks with your burgers?"

"Of course. Two colas."

"Is this to stay or to go?"

"We're eating here."

She punched a few more buttons.

"That'll be $30.87."

Emily took out her credit card and tapped on a machine to pay. She grabbed a plastic card with her order number from the cashier and led Eric back to a cozy booth in the dining area. His lips formed a slight pout as they approached their table.

"What's wrong?" she asked.

"Don't call me sweetie in front of people from school." Eric glanced quickly over his shoulder at the counter. "It's embarrassing."

Emily furrowed her brows. A half-frown appeared on her face.

"Show me a mother who doesn't call her son sweetie," she said. "Besides, I don't think the girl taking our order will like you any less."

"What?" His eyes widened and his voice dropped to a virtual whisper. "I don't like Jenna. She's dating Brock."

"Brock … he also plays on the basketball team, right?"

"Yeah, he does. And Jenna's a blabbermouth. I'll bet anything Brock will start calling me 'sweetie' tomorrow."

Emily looked down and away. She sometimes forgot how being a teenager meant dealing with stupid shit from equally stupid peers. It bugged her to know a term of endearment to her son could be thrown back in his face if heard by the wrong person.

She slid into her booth seat.

"I didn't mean to embarrass you," Emily said.

Eric dropped down into the seat across from her. He met her gaze again after setting his phone on the table.

"If this Brock kid is hassling you," Emily continued. "Maybe you should tell your coach or the principal —"

"The principal?"

A definite sharpness rose in his voice. Emily realized she made a terrible suggestion as soon as the words left her tongue. Principal Reynolds couldn't be counted on to do anything to make Eric's situation better. All those earlier meetings in her office proved as much. That pompous disagreeable woman would only accuse him of inviting verbal jabs from the other kids.

Her attitude made Emily want to deliver a different type of jab with her fists.

"Scratch that last suggestion," she said. "I forgot for a moment who we're dealing with."

Eric shrugged.

"It's okay, Mom." His eyes drifted over to the napkin dispenser. "Nothing I can't handle."

Jenna approached their table with a serving tray holding two plates with burgers and steak fries and two glasses filled to the brim with cola. She set the rancher's choice burger in front of Eric and the bacon cheeseburger in front of Emily.

"Do you need anything else?" Jenna asked after setting the two sodas down on the table.

Emily glanced over at Eric. He had scooped up his phone and buried his face in the screen again. His efforts to avoid talking to this specific classmate at all costs were painfully obvious.

"I think we're good," she said.

Jenna cast a cursory glance at Eric. Her eyes darted back to Emily, and she smiled and nodded. She left with the empty serving tray. Eric's face shot up from his phone again as soon as Jenna was out of earshot.

His eyes fell on his plate.

"She didn't bring any ketchup for my fries."

Emily glanced down and instantly noticed the same absence of ketchup on her plate. She pressed her lips together and released an irritated sigh.

"I'll flag her down and get some."

She sprang out of her seat and dashed after Jenna, catching up to her as she passed a garbage basket.

"Could you bring us some ketchup?" she asked, tapping the teen on the shoulder. "Neither of us were given any with our fries."

Jenna flashed a tight-lipped smile. Emily wasn't certain if the girl was annoyed at messing up their order or annoyed a customer pointed out her mistake.

"I'll take care of it right away," Jenna said.

Emily thanked her and wheeled around. She took a step right into another customer who had been crossing behind her. A tall to-go soda cup popped out of his right hand. Ice and root beer splattered all over the floor.

Emily pressed her lips together and rubbed her hands over her cheeks. She reached down to grab his cup.

"I'm so sorry," she said. "I didn't see you behind me."

The other customer — a tall and handsome brown-haired man — raised a hand and smiled.

"No worries," he said. "Accidents happen. I probably need to cut down on my daily pop intake anyway."

Emily handed the cup back to the brown-haired man. His eyes featured a matching brown hue.

"Let me make up for it," she said. "Let's get another soda — my treat."

He glanced down at the cup and her hand. The brown-haired man met her eyes again and quickly shook his head.

"You can make it up to me by getting a coffee with me later," he said.

Did he just check out her ring finger to see if she was married? Emily followed his eyes to see if he was also checking her out. She responded to his suggestion with a slight smirk.

"I'm new in town," he said. "Moved out here for a job and haven't had a chance to really meet anyone outside of work yet. Maybe you could give me the lowdown on Deer Falls."

"I enjoy an occasional espresso," she said. "I know a spot around here that brews a decent one."

"Great. Let me get your number and we can meet up for that killer espresso."

Emily's smile deepened and she motioned for his smartphone. The brown-haired man dug his phone out of his pocket, swiped the screen, and handed it to her. She punched her first name and number into his contacts and then gave the phone back to him.

"Thank you, Emily," he said. "I'll call or text you as soon as I return home."

Her future coffee date started past her.

"Wait," Emily said. "What's your name?"

He turned and flashed a smile at her, adding a brief polite laugh.

"Here I am, getting so excited thinking about coffee that I nearly forgot to introduce myself."

He drew closer to Emily again and offered his hand.

"My name is Robb. Robb Cooper."

11

Eric peeked at the scoreboard on his way to the bench during the timeout. Sweat dripped from his brow. Deer Falls trailed Skyline by four points with a minute left and had the ball. Coach Watkins stood before the team and drew up an inbounds play on his clipboard. A door hung open to complete a successful rally. All the Bucks needed was two or three baskets — and a stop or two along the way — to prevail.

Victory over a favored opponent lay within reach.

"It's on you," Watkins said, pointing to Eric as the team broke their sideline huddle. "Just get a clean inbounds pass to Trace and let him go to work."

Eric nodded and took his place next to the official holding the ball. The official tossed the ball to him and blew his whistle. A defender along the sideline flailed his arms in front of Eric, trying to obstruct his vision and force a bad pass or a five-second violation. Eric threaded the ball past his outstretched arm to Trace. The Bucks' point guard dribbled around a screen and cut to the rim for a layup. Raucous cheers rippled through the entire Deer Falls student section when the ball dropped through the hoop.

His basket cut Skyline's lead down to two points.

Eric hung back with Trace and Devin after the basket. The trio applied a full court press against Skyline's point guard. He threw the

81

ball right into Devin's waiting hands, eliciting another roar from the home crowd. Devin hit a streaking Trace for a second layup.

Tie game.

Skyline timeout with 37 seconds left.

Eric exchanged high-fives with Devin on their way back to the bench. Deer Falls had pinned the Falcons against the ropes, ready to deliver a final knockout blow.

"We've got this," Brock said in the team huddle. "They can't handle our defense."

Coach Watkins instructed his players to stick with the full court press. He didn't want Skyline to dribble the clock down and get a clean look at a game-winner. When they broke the huddle again, Eric positioned himself at a spot near the halfcourt line.

A Falcons' player tossed an inbounds pass to a teammate near Eric. He blanketed him and tried to trap the other player along the sideline. Brock deflected a panicked pass into the backcourt. Eric sprinted after the ball with a Skyline player hot on his tail. He scooped it up and drove for the rim — intending to score a go-ahead layup. A hard shove in his back sent Eric tumbling to the floor. The referee nearest to him blew his whistle and turned to the scorer's table.

"Foul on 22. Two shots."

Eric gulped. Two free throws would complete their rally and put Deer Falls ahead.

His free throws.

He stepped to the line and took a calming breath. The referee bounced him the ball. Eric spun it in his hand, dribbled twice, and released the ball.

It rimmed out.

His heart raced faster as Eric sized up the second free throw attempt. He tried to calm himself and visualize the ball going through the hoop.

It left his hand and bounced off the back iron.

A Skyline player boxed out and snared the rebound. He chucked an outlet pass to a teammate sprinting past the halfcourt line. No one from Deer Falls got back on defense fast enough to impede his path to the basket. The Falcons' player charged to the rim and threw down an easy dunk as the final seconds ticked away.

Game over.

Deer Falls lost by two points.

Eric avoided eye contact with Skyline players and coaches while shuffling through the postgame handshake line. He mumbled "good game" repeatedly and kept his head down. His team lost because he choked on the free throw line at the worst possible moment. A huge upset victory slipped from their grasp because of his failure. Eric wanted to crawl deep under a rock and stay hidden until everyone forgot about the game.

Especially his teammates.

Most were sympathetic in the locker room after the game. Devin repeatedly tried to reassure Eric that his missed free throws didn't cost them the game like a good friend should do. Brock and Trace were a different story. Sour glares were tattooed on their faces as two sets of hardened eyes locked on him.

Eric tried to ignore both teens while he showered and dressed. Their body language told him nothing they had to say deserved his time or energy. Neither teammate approached his locker while he showered and dressed. When Eric grabbed his phone and pushed the locker door shut, however, he found himself standing face-to-face with Trace.

"Maybe you should stay after practice and learn how to shoot free throws," Trace said. "I knew sooner or later you'd cost us a game."

Eric sidestepped him.

"I don't want to talk about it," he said. "I'm not in the mood to deal with your bullshit."

Trace circled from behind Eric and blocked his path.

"I'm not letting this drop." He stabbed an index finger at him. "When are you going to take basketball more seriously? The rest of us want to win a state title. How about you?"

"Who says I don't take basketball seriously?" Eric scowled and crossed his arms. "I work my ass off in practice just like everyone else."

"Really? You're last in the gym and first to leave every day."

"Who in the hell do you think you are?"

"I'm the fucking team captain," Trace's voice climbed a couple of decibels. "And I was chosen for a reason. It's my job to keep us all on the same page and playing for each other like a band of brothers."

"So, my missed free throws disrupt team chemistry," Eric shot back. "Is that what you're saying?"

Eric's cheeks grew flushed. His brows knitted together. What Trace left unsaid caught his attention more than all the nonsense spewing from his lips during his cliche spouting tirade.

He didn't want him playing on the team.

Eric suspected as much when they both made the varsity roster last season. Trace didn't have the same authority as a senior leader did to impose his will. Once he got voted team captain heading into this season, the odds shifted in his favor. Eric didn't need mind-reading powers to know he was no longer welcome on the team.

Too damn bad. Trace wasn't getting his way.

"I'm not quitting," he said. "You're stuck with me the whole season."

Eric cut past him a second time and headed for the door leading out to the main gym. Sensing Trace trying to push past him, he stuck his arm out toward the white brick wall.

"We're not done here," Trace said.

Eric glanced back when he pushed open the door and stared hard at his teammate.

"Wanna bet?"

He turned and marched into the gym. Scattered fans and students still lingered around the bleachers. Some cleaned up discarded game programs and food wrappers. Others engaged in idle conversation.

Trace caught up to Eric again at the bleachers.

"You've always had a screw loose since middle school," he said. "Your head isn't in the game and it's weighing my whole team down."

Eric stopped under the hoop and wheeled around. His lips curled into a deep scowl.

"What's that supposed to mean?"

"I haven't forgotten about your freshman year screaming fit in home room." He mimed rubbing his eyes like they were filled with tears. "Boo Hoo. An imaginary witch tried to kill me."

Eric let out a shout and lunged at Trace. He tackled him with furious energy. The two teens became a jumble of arms and legs on the court. Eric tried to lock his arm around Trace's throat in a choke hold. He recoiled and gasped when Trace thrust an elbow into his gut.

"That's enough! Stop it!"

A pair of stout arms seized Eric from behind and jerked him to his feet. Those same arms spun him around until he faced a tall brown-haired man with a squared jaw. The man's brown eyes narrowed and bored into Eric as firmly as his hands held him in place. Heavy breaths escaped Eric's lips while he silently cursed his bad luck.

He stood face to face with Robb Cooper — the high school's new assistant principal. Principal Reynolds introduced Cooper during a brief early morning assembly last month. Eric did not relish the thought of dealing with her new sidekick so soon.

Trace scrambled to his feet. His hair was disheveled from the brief scuffle, but he bore no visible bruises. Eric also suffered no bruises.

"What do you boys have to say for yourselves?" Cooper's stern tone perfectly matched his words. "Such violent behavior has no place in this school."

Eric dipped his chin and gnawed on his lower lip. Both eyes settled on the floor and stayed fixed to a spot in front of his sneakers. He dared not make eye contact with Cooper. Why did he lose his cool? Principal Reynolds craved the smallest excuse to suspend or expel him. Fighting with Trace simply gift-wrapped one to her on a silver platter.

What would his mom think?

Emily went to bat for him a zillion times in the past. Eric despaired at the thought he broke her faith at a critical moment.

"What do you want me to say?" Trace shot back. "He tackled me. I was only defending myself."

"Nice try," Cooper said. "I heard what you said. It doesn't condone his behavior, but you're certainly no damned angel here."

Eric lifted his head and glanced over at Trace. His teammate sported a visibly frustrated pout. He had grown accustomed to teachers and administrators showering him with preferential treatment because he was the starting point guard.

"We have a zero-tolerance policy for fighting," Cooper continued. "I'll inform your coach tomorrow morning and recommend you both serve a one-game suspension."

Trace's eyes widened. He pressed his lips together like he was trying to stifle tears from escaping in front of the new assistant principal.

Eric answered with a resigned nod.

"I'm sorry I lost my temper," he said. "I won't let it happen again."

Trace showed no contrition for his role in egging on Eric's attack.

"You can't do this to me," he said. "When I tell my dad about this, he'll make you regret taking a job here."

Eric snapped his head back at his teammate. His eyes widened and he stared at him unblinking. Threatening an assistant principal wasn't a smart idea. Did Trace want to extend his suspension to include school days too?

"Is that a fact, son?"

11

Cooper crossed his arms. An irritated frown followed. His body language confirmed Eric's suspicions. Trace only threatened to create added trouble for himself in the form of a stiffer punishment. Facing that possible outcome didn't deter him from running his mouth.

"My uncle is a partner in a major Denver law firm," Trace said. "My dad will turn him loose on you. Once my uncle is done digging dirt on you, and sues you for everything you own, you'll beg me for mercy."

Cooper's eyes hardened but he also visibly swallowed hard at Trace's threats. He glared at the teen. A tense silence settled inside the gym. Eric's eyes darted over to the bleachers. Other students had paused their activities and conversations. Several pairs of eyes now fixed on them, watching with great interest as their uncomfortable confrontation unfolded.

The extra attention did not escape Cooper's notice. He let out a curt sigh and adjusted a cuff on the sleeve of his collared shirt.

"Fix your attitude or you'll be facing more than a one-game suspension," he said.

"Talk to my dad and my uncle," Trace shot back. "I've got nothing else to say."

He stormed away before the assistant principal said another word and flung open the gym doors. Cooper stared at the doors for a moment after they slammed shut, shook his head, and walked away from Eric without saying another word.

Trace's behavior promised to buy him a longer suspension. Or so Eric hoped. He deserved it after everything he said. Eric decided to play it safe and head home before the assistant principal chose to also lengthen his suspension beyond a single game.

12

Robb excused himself from the gymnasium when that mouthy teen ran off in mid-tantrum. Lora warned him about a handful of troublemakers during his first-day orientation. Trace claimed a spot near the top of her unofficial shit list. Teachers walked on eggshells around him because his uncle's law firm successfully sued the school district in the past. This led to a teacher being fired over a disciplinary action she took against the teen. A scapegoat to help the district save face.

Trace offered Robb a much different reason to feel concerned. Which Denver law firm did his uncle work for as a partner?

One specific firm — Crowley & Flanagan — represented clients affiliated with the Order of the Crimson Thorns. If Trace's uncle practiced with the same firm, then the mouthy teen had the means to seriously disrupt his careful plan against the Order.

Robb whipped out his smartphone and brought up Crowley & Flanagan's homepage. A quick scroll through partner listings revealed an entry for Gordon Fowler. His photo showed a definite familial resemblance to Trace. Same jawline. Similar blue eyes.

Bad news.

Extremely bad news.

"I can't let this seed sprout," Robb mumbled.

He glanced down at the silver chain circling his neck. Robb clasped the amulet concealed below his shirt, wrapping his fingers around fabric. He stared at his hand and hesitated for a moment. Far too little time had passed since he drained life energy from that phony psychic and her boyfriend. Another death now might arouse suspicion and draw unwanted attention.

Trace left him no choice.

Robb couldn't afford to leave anything to chance. His eyelids snapped shut and he focused his mind on tapping into latent powers dwelling within the life energy he absorbed a month earlier.

Tell me where to find Trace Fowler.

A warmth passed through his hand and traveled up his arm. Soon, a distinct image flashed through his mind bearing the clarity and sharpness of a video feed. Trace exited from the school and, with eyes downward, walked toward the senior parking lot. Breath escaped from his lips as visible wisps. Both thumbs tapped a smartphone screen furiously as he fired off texts.

The teen's image vanished again as quickly as it first appeared. Robb's eyelids snapped open.

"Bingo. Found you."

He marched down the hall and headed for the same exit Trace used earlier. Robb stopped at the art room and twisted the doorknob. It did not budge.

Locked.

With one hand clasping the amulet, Robb pressed his index finger against the keyhole and closed his eyelids.

Reserare.

The same warmth rushed from the amulet up through his arm and crossed over to the other arm. Robb opened his eyes again. A spark flew from his finger through the keyhole and the lock turned on the other side.

He marched into the room and wrenched off a guillotine-style blade from a paper cutter. Robb shoved the foot-long blade inside the belt line on his pants and resumed his march down the hall toward the parking lot.

Robb surveyed the lot as soon as he stepped outside. He spotted a teen's head adorned with frosted tips ducking into a car about ten yards away from him. Trace hadn't left the school grounds quite yet.

Robb intended to keep it that way.

He sprinted up to the car as the engine started. Robb slowed to a walk as he approached the driver's side door and knocked on the window. Trace turned and jumped in his seat.

"Turn off the engine." He motioned for the teen to roll down his window. "We're not done talking."

Trace scowled and shook his head.

"I'm not supposed to talk to you," he said. "The only one who will be talking to you now is my uncle."

Robb sighed. No wonder Lora hated his guts. This little brat deserved the fate looming over him.

"Gordon Fowler?"

Trace furrowed his brow. He glanced down at his phone's screen and back at him.

"How do you know my uncle?"

"Thank you." Robb's mouth twisted into a crooked smile. "You just confirmed my suspicions."

He drew back his arm and punched his fist through the window. Trace's eyes widened and he unleashed a terrified shout. Broken glass fell into his lap and struck his chest. The teen gulped and instantly shifted the car into reverse.

Robb shook his head.

"You're not getting away from me that easily."

He clutched the amulet concealed under his shirt again and uttered an incantation. The gear shifter knob moved on its own from reverse back into park. Trace tugged on it, but the knob refused to move. His eyes darted from the knob to Robb's clenched fist.

Not even a slight scratch or trace of blood showed on the exposed skin of his hand. The teen's lips trembled. Tears rolled down his cheeks. Robb withdrew his arm through the broken window and his smile deepened.

"I reconsidered your punishment and decided a one-game suspension isn't enough," he said. "More drastic measures are needed to teach you a lesson."

"Who are you?" Fear choked Trace's voice. "How can you punch through glass like that?"

Robb shrugged.

"I'm invulnerable. A nice little spell I cast to protect me until I've done what I must do. Nothing can leave behind so much as a scratch, scrape, or bruise."

"Please don't hurt me," Trace begged, sniffling back new tears. "I won't talk to my uncle. I promise."

"I don't believe you," Robb said. "Even if I did, I don't negotiate with children."

He drew out the paper cutter blade and smashed out more glass with a swing at the broken window. Trace screamed. His fingers fumbled with his seatbelt release. Once the belt popped free, he lunged toward the passenger's seat.

Robb wrenched open the car door.

A second swing brought down the blade on Trace's left arm. Sharpened metal sliced through his jacket sleeve and penetrated flesh underneath the fabric. Blood spurted out from a deep gash along his wrist. His hand dangled, partially severed from the forearm.

Trace screamed and crawled over the cup holders, extending his uninjured arm toward the passenger side door. He knocked his phone off the seat. It landed on the floor mat with a thud.

Robb ducked inside the car and took a third swing.

This time, the blade found Trace's neck.

Half of his ear fell into the nearest cup holder. Blood gushed from his jaw and neck. Trace sobbed. Two of his fingers curled around the door handle.

Robb dropped the blade and drew out the reaper amulet from under his shirt collar. He seized Trace by the shoulder and pulled him upward toward the driver's side door. Once Trace's bloodied head drew close enough to the amulet, he pressed it against the teen's forehead.

A shimmering glow flowed from Trace into Robb. He drew in a sharp breath as this burst of life energy surged through every vein and artery. Robb relaxed his grip and let the teen's lifeless body sink back into the driver's seat.

"So much sheer power." He licked his lips and savored what he had consumed. "God, it's amazing. I feel almost superhuman."

Everything Robb read about the Reaper Amulet pointed to such an outcome. Drawing out life energy from seven individuals promised the possessor of the amulet unrivaled powers. They gained greater power with each energy absorption. It sounded like an impossible myth in the beginning. Now after consuming life energy from three victims, Robb began to truly understand that the powers connected to the amulet were quite real. Once he fully unlocked these powers, the entire Order would fall before him. Survivors would fall to their knees and pledge eternal loyalty to Robb alone.

When that wonderful day arrived, he would rule both heaven and hell unopposed.

Snowflakes plastered Robb and the car when he retreated to a standing position by the driver's side door again. Robb studied the crime scene. He needed to work quickly before a bystander had a chance to walk out into the parking lot, come across the dead teen, and put all the pieces together.

He ducked inside a second time. Robb leaned over the fresh corpse and retrieved Trace's phone from the floor mat in front of the passenger seat. He also grabbed the bloodied paper cutter blade. Robb stuffed the phone in his jacket pocket and set the blade on the car roof.

Making it look like the teen perished in a fiery car crash wouldn't be a simple task. Robb had no other options where he could destroy evidence with equal speed and thoroughness.

He closed the door and grabbed the blade again. Robb repeated the incantation controlling the gear shifter knob. It moved back into reverse. Robb stuck the blade inside his belt and walked to the front bumper. Planting both hands on the grill, he pushed the car backward until the vehicle had enough space to turn out of the lot. Robb jogged over to the driver side door again and said the incantation a third time. This time around, the vehicle shifted into drive. Robb guided Trace's car through the parking lot, pushing it toward the street running from north to south in front of the school. When the car reached the open gate, he uttered a different incantation.

Trace's right leg suddenly jerked forward. His foot pressed down on the gas pedal. The car peeled out of the lot and slammed headfirst into a utility pole directly across the street from the school. Metal buckled across the front end, twisting it like a pretzel. A power line snapped and swung down toward the vehicle. It touched a stream of gas leaking from under the car.

A spark ignited a trail of flames, retreating to the vehicle. Within a few seconds, a voracious fire spread from hood to trunk. It consumed metal and upholstery with an insatiable hunger. Flames encircled Trace and devoured his lifeless flesh and bone with the same zeal.

Lights extinguished up and down the street. The high school and neighboring residences all simultaneously plunged into darkness. Robb let out a relieved sigh and walked away from the flaming wreckage.

He still needed to clean himself up. Dispose of his bloody clothes and the murder weapon in a place where no one would be able to find them. Time favored Robb. Once power had been restored to the block, Trace and his car would be reduced to nothing more than a pile of twisted, blackened metal and ashes.

Robb wore a satisfied smile as he approached his car in the teacher's lot. Snowflakes tumbled from shadowy clouds in greater abundance around him. Only one thing left to do to finish staging this accident.

He pulled out Trace's smartphone from his pocket and swiped the screen to keep it from going black. Robb retrieved the teen's text messages and saw the most recent one had been sent to Trace's father.

Heading home. Feeling a little tired.

Robb pressed send. Three dots appeared below.

Be careful driving home. Love you.

He chuckled and then tossed the phone aside on the passenger seat. Draining life energy from a brat harboring an indirect connection to The Order only made this journey more rewarding. He had encountered minor complications along the way, but Robb prided himself on his ability to adapt to changing circumstances while still executing his plan.

Now only four individuals stood in his way.

13

Eric's mouth dropped open. He slumped down and sat unmoving at the bottom of the stairs. A numb shock blanketed him from head to toe. What his mom said didn't feel real or possible. Trace was still alive when he left the gym after their scuffle last night. This morning, his teammate was dead.

A victim of a crash burnt to a crisp inside his car.

"I'm so sorry, honey," Emily sat on the same stair next to him. "I know he was your teammate and friend."

Eric glanced over at her and swallowed hard.

"He wasn't my friend. But, at the same time, I didn't want him to drop dead."

He gnawed on his lower lip and turned away. Eric's eyes drifted to his feet, tracing the outline of his sneakers. His mom wrapped her arm around his back, pressing her hand against his opposite shoulder.

"It's happening again, isn't it?" he asked. "She found a way to escape her chest."

"Cassandra isn't coming back."

"How can you feel so certain? This is how everything started last time. Random brutal killings."

"Your sister-in-law is powerful with magic. Christina says she made it impossible for Cassandra to ever return. I believe her."

Eric pinched his eyes shut. He wanted to believe Christina too.

Continual nightmarish hallucinations after she and Ron buried the chest near Keg Hill had shaken his faith.

Trace's death was no accident. Eric refused to accept such a notion. No bad thing in Deer Falls ever happened by accident. His death raised Eric's suspicions. If someone killed Trace, that made him the third known murder victim in their town in the past month. This stood out as more than a simple coincidence. Still, if Christina's magic was as irreversible as his mom insisted, this latest death opened a door to another frightening possibility.

"What if a different evil witch is the one going on a new killing spree?" he asked.

Eric only heard a sudden gasp from his mom. He cast his eyes up at her. Color drained from Emily's face as though she had seen a ghost.

"God, I hope not."

A brief tremor gripped her voice as she uttered those four words. His mom did her best to put on a brave face around him, especially during times when Eric struggled with hallucinations. But she couldn't quite conceal her own trauma, no matter how hard she tried.

Cassandra kidnapped Emily six years ago and encased her in vines on a bed. The vines ran from her feet to her neck and were designed to drain away her life force in an incremental, painful fashion. Eric had his near-death encounter with the witch specifically because he tracked down his mom and tried to free her from the vines by cutting through each one with a steak knife.

The same steak knife Cassandra attempted to impale into his chest when she seized control of Eric's arm using her dark magic.

"Let's leave Deer Falls," he said. "Pack up tonight."

Her eyes locked on his own.

"You make it sound easier than it is."

"Can't we go stay with Uncle Steve and Aunt Joanna? They'd welcome us."

Emily looked away and fixed her gaze on the front door. A defeated smile appeared on her lips.

"Small house. Four kids — all younger than you. It would be a catastrophe waiting to happen."

"Beats staying here waiting to …"

He trailed off. Eric couldn't bring himself to complete the sentence. Die.

The word stayed silent on his lips. Still, his mom had to know what he meant. Staying here in Deer Falls amounted to a death sentence. If a new witch, or demon, or monster had embarked on a killing spree, time wasn't on their side. Sooner or later, they would turn their attention to Eric, his mom, and his friends. After what happened six years ago, Eric doubted he possessed enough mental strength to endure another battle with supernatural forces.

A loud knock came at the door. Emily kissed Eric on the forehead and rose to her feet. She walked to the door. When his mom glanced through the peephole, she let out an irritated sigh.

"Not him," she muttered.

Emily opened the door, revealing Sheriff Leeds standing on the other side. He greeted her with a brisk nod. His breath billowed out in visible wisps.

"Can I help you with something, Sheriff?" Emily's annoyance threaded through her voice.

"Do you mind if I come in?" Leeds wiped his boots on the welcome mat, kicking fresh snow off his toes. "It's a bit chilly out here."

She beckoned him forward. He brushed snowflakes off the front of his black coat and stepped inside. Emily closed the front door behind him. The sheriff blew on his hands and flashed an appreciative smile.

"What do you want?"

"I need to talk to your son." Leeds glanced at the stairs and gave Eric a cursory nod. "I have a few questions for him."

"Questions? About what?"

"A student died under suspicious circumstances near the high school last night. We're hoping your boy can clear a few things up for us."

Eric's muscles stiffened and he swallowed hard. Of course, Leeds suspected he played a part in Trace's death. Someone must have told him about their scuffle in the gym after the game.

"My son had nothing to do with the Fowler boy's death." Emily's voice grew firm. "He came straight home after last night's game because of the snowstorm."

Leeds pulled out a reporter's notebook and pen from his front coat pocket. He flipped open the notebook and clicked the pen.

"Humor me," he said, fixing his eyes on Eric.

Eric didn't move from his spot on the stairs. He leaned forward, resting his wrists on his knees.

"I'll talk — as long as my mom stays in the room."

Leeds let out a whispered sigh.

"Fine with me."

He approached the stairs and rested his arm on the banister. Leeds never shifted his eyes away from Eric for a second.

"I understand you and Trace Fowler got into a little skirmish in the gym following last night's game," he said. "Is that correct?"

Eric hung his head and stared at his shoes for a moment. He hadn't told his mom about the fight yet. This wasn't how he wanted to break the news.

"Yeah, we had a scuffle."

He lifted his chin and glimpsed a disapproving frown from Emily. Eric quickly averted his eyes from his mom back to Leeds. The sheriff jotted his answer down in the notebook.

"Witnesses in the gym told me you suddenly tackled him," Leeds said, making eye contact with him again. "Why did you do that, son?"

"We were arguing in the locker room. Trace kept berating me over a pair of late free throws I missed."

"Your reaction makes me think this confrontation became more personal than a beef over foul shots."

"He made fun of me over a hallucination I had in one of our freshman year classes. It made me mad."

Leeds jotted down additional notes. He tapped the pen against the open page when he finished and studied Eric with a piercing stare.

"Mad enough to follow Trace out to the parking lot? Mad enough to confront him a second time?"

Emily circled in front of Eric and faced the sheriff. He glimpsed a distinct fire in his mom's eyes before she turned her back to him.

"Are you accusing my son of murder?" The fury in her voice perfectly matched Emily's expression. "That's a damned lie and you know damn well it is. How dare you make such an unfounded accusation?"

Leeds clipped his pen to the notebook and motioned for her to step off to the side.

"Trace Fowler died shortly after having a public confrontation with your son," he said. "If you don't find that scenario suspicious, then you're the only one."

"Why do you think someone murdered him?" she shot back. "Once again, we had a snowstorm last night. Roads get icy in heavy snow and lead to crashes. People die in car crashes all the time."

What his mom said made sense. Still, Eric shared the sheriff's skepticism. Driving conditions weren't nearly bad enough around the high school when he left to cause a car crash. Someone staged Trace's death to look like a tragic accident.

The evidence pointed to him.

Eric needed to clear his name quickly before Leeds slapped a pair of handcuffs on his wrists and hauled him off to jail. He was no murderer. That distinction belonged exclusively to Cassandra and others like her.

"I didn't kill Trace," he said. "I never talked to him once he stormed out of the gym."

"What did you do after he left?" Leeds asked.

"I texted my friends on a group text and then texted my mom," Eric replied. "Then, I headed to my car and drove home."

"You parked in the senior lot — same as the Fowler boy?"

"Yeah. All the seniors park there."

Leeds unclipped his pen from the notebook. A click followed. He quickly scribbled down new notes.

"Wait." Eric held up his hand. "His car was still in the lot when I left. I saw Trace walking in that direction when I backed up and drove out of the lot."

The sheriff glanced up from his notebook.

"Did you see anyone else with him or following him?"

He shook his head.

Leeds furrowed his brow. His eyes hardened and stayed fixed on Eric for a moment. They finally slid back to the notebook. He flipped to an earlier page and held it up to Eric.

"What can you tell me about this symbol?"

A hand drawn cross greeted his eyes. At least Eric thought it was a cross. It had the correct shape, but the bars were unlike anything he'd ever seen. Both resembled scythe blades.

'I've never seen this before," he said, making eye contact with Leeds again. "What is it? What does it have to do with Trace's death?"

The sheriff pinched his lips together, ignoring Eric's questions. He stuck the notebook and pen back in his coat pocket. Emily gave him a sideways glance.

"What aren't you telling us?" she asked. "Is some kind of supernatural entity connected to this crash?"

Leeds clucked his tongue and fought to suppress an irritated smile.

"Why do you ask?" he shot back. "Are you searching for material to include in your next novel?"

The sheriff turned and started for the door. Emily rolled her eyes and shook her head.

"You know, I wasn't the only one who got into an argument with Trace," Eric said. "He also threatened our new assistant principal."

Leeds stopped and wheeled around. His eyes narrowed and he drew out his pen and notebook from his pocket a second time.

"What did he say?"

Eric scratched his head.

"The assistant principal told us he'd suspend us from playing in our next game for fighting. Trace freaked out and threatened to get his uncle to sue him."

Leeds raised his eyebrows and tightened his lips. He jotted down this latest revelatory nugget in his notebook.

"Thank you." He glanced up at Eric after stashing the notebook away again. "I'll let you know if I have any further questions."

The sheriff gave Emily a polite nod and let himself out through the front door. Questions flooded into Eric's mind after the door closed behind him. What did that strange cross symbol mean? How was it connected to Trace's death? Leeds refused to share any helpful details, so Eric had only one other choice.

Uncovering the answers himself.

Someone decided to follow in Cassandra's footsteps. Their plans must be thwarted — no matter what cost came from opposing this new foe. Eric's instincts told him not to get involved this time. He would only endanger himself again. Staying on the sidelines wasn't an option, though, no matter how much he wanted it to be one.

Living in a town as screwed up as Deer Falls left no room for enjoying a normal life.

14

All these years later, the decrepit Graber house occupied the same lot unmoved and unchanged. Frozen in time. An enduring monument to a single nightmarish night Eric failed to cleanse from his memory no matter how hard he scrubbed. Thick plywood boards covered empty spaces that windows and an oak door once occupied. A broken beam lay across the front porch.

Remnants from a battle for survival against a dark entity bent on his destruction. A battle he scarcely won.

Why did no one bother to tear this eyesore down?

An answer entered his mind almost as soon as Eric posed the internal question. For sale signs came and went since that awful night without drawing a serious buyer. No person in their right mind wanted to own a house where so many people met a gruesome end. He didn't blame them for a second. The house carried a dark curse. Why tempt fate and try to remodel or rebuild?

Eric pushed down his bike's kickstand with the top of his sneaker and left it to linger in the driveway. His feet crunched over alternating patches of brown grass and snow. He paused in the center of the long-dead lawn and craned his neck skyward.

Had she returned?

Did Cassandra spy on him from the place she called home for a brief time? Or did someone else equally nightmarish skulk around up there?

The idea of a new killer fitting her same sadistic mold roaming around Deer Falls made Eric's blood run ice cold.

"I don't think hanging out here is the best idea."

Eric nearly jumped out of his skin at the sound of Max's voice. He snapped his head in his best friend's direction. Max parked a few steps behind the rear tire of Eric's bike and hopped off his own bicycle. His eyes settled on the house's second floor, and he pinched his lips tight looking like he wanted to stifle a scream.

"What if she came back?" Eric turned away from Max again. His eyes trailed back to the same spot as earlier. "She did it twice before, you know."

"No. History won't repeat. I refuse to believe it."

A rare sharpness cut through Max's voice. Eric answered him with a worried sigh and glanced over at his friend a second time.

"My mom agrees with you."

"You should listen to her."

Eric stared past his shoulder at the two bicycles and frowned. Max made such a choice sound far too simple. He wished for a simple life filled with simple choices. Life repeatedly told him a different story.

"Sheriff Leeds came over to my house on Saturday." He returned his gaze to Max. "Asked a ton of questions about Trace — mostly about our fight after the game."

Max flashed a puzzled frown.

"Why? What does that have to do with Trace going out and slamming his car into a pole?"

"I think the sheriff figures I killed him."

"That's stupid."

"Tell me about it. But he shared a detail that stuck with me. I can't get it out of my head."

Max's brows pulled together, and his eyes formed a partial squint.

"What detail?"

"He showed me a strange symbol — a weird-looking cross." Eric traced an invisible cross with his fingers. "It looked like two scythe blades formed the cross."

His friend's frown deepened.

"What is it supposed —"

"I have no clue what it's supposed to mean." Eric said, anticipating the question he cut off. "But I bet that symbol is tied to Trace's death somehow. And we better find out what the connection is."

Max cast his eyes down at his sneakers.

"I'm not ready to go through this again."

"Neither am I," Eric said. "What choice do we have?"

Both teens mounted their bicycles again and pedaled away from the Graber house. A brisk breeze pounded Eric's cheeks as they turned out of Willow Flats. Fresh worried thoughts buffeted him with equal force and persistence. He didn't know where to start with digging up any useful information on the mysterious symbol. They needed help from someone far more knowledgeable in supernatural lore.

Only one person met those qualifications.

Eric led Max back to his house. The place was empty when he opened the front door. He poked his head inside his mom's office. A darkened laptop screen and empty office chair greeted him.

"Mom?" Eric backed out of the office. His eyes darted from wall to wall as he called out to her. "Are you home?"

No response. He glanced inside the kitchen. A large note was posted to the refrigerator door. Eric walked over to the refrigerator and yanked the paper out from under a Pizza Wagon magnet.

A message from his mom.

Out on a lunch date. Help yourself to the leftovers in the fridge.

"Lunch date?" Eric wondered aloud. "I thought Mom threw in the towel on dating."

Who was the mystery guy? Eric stared at her note for a few extra seconds before finally shaking his head. He dropped the paper on the counter and walked away. Bigger concerns loomed in front of him.

Eric led Max up to his room and booted up his laptop. He clicked on a video calling app and dialed the first saved number. A screen popped up and his brother's face appeared.

"What's new, little bro?"

Ron flashed one of his trademark annoying smirks at him. Eric didn't return the smile.

"Something really troublesome."

"Can it wait?" Ron turned and glanced behind his shoulder. "You caught me at a bad time. I'm just heading out the door to practice."

Eric glimpsed a zipped-up tote bag behind him sitting on the bed. It bore a Real Monarchs logo on the side facing the laptop camera.

"Is Christina there?"

"She left for her shift about a half-hour ago. What do you need? I'm sure I can help if it doesn't chew up a bunch of time."

Eric paused and cast a side-eye glance over at Max. Ron had dealt with the supernatural of course, but still did not know enough about supernatural things to offer any meaningful help. What they were dealing with in Deer Falls called for Christina's expertise.

"What do you know about scythe blade crosses?" he finally asked, deciding to give him the benefit of the doubt. "That symbol turned up on a teammate who died in a car accident a few days ago."

Ron scrunched up his face at Eric's question and then pursed his lips.

"I'll let her know you called," he said. "Gotta go."

His face vanished from the video screen. Eric snapped his head over to Max and expressed his irritation with a deep sigh.

"He hasn't changed at all," Max said.

Ron's abrupt departure left them with only one other option. Eric didn't trust his brother to remember to pass the message on to Christina later. It wouldn't be the first time he neglected something that offered no personal importance to him. Until Eric finally had a chance to pick her brain, it fell on him and Max to try to figure out this shit on their own.

* * *

Monday afternoons were the worst. Robb kept checking the digital clock on his desk against his better judgment. Minutes and seconds crawled by at a snail's pace while he pored over a stack of teacher evaluations. All the files were already on his laptop, but Robb convinced himself that printing out hard copies and reading through them by hand would be quicker and easier. It only took reading through a handful of evaluations before choosing that route felt like an annoying mistake.

Robb plunked his pen down on the desk and leaned back in his chair. He clasped his arms behind his head and closed his eyelids. Walking around and stretching his legs would do a world of good.

"Robb?"

Knuckles wrapped against his office door. His eyes snapped open. Lora stood in the doorway. The principal wore a polite smile. One that contrasted sharply with a serious look lingering in her eyes. He instantly leaned forward and brought his arms down to his desk.

"What can I do for you?"

"We need to chat for a minute."

"About what?"

Lora glanced over her shoulder and quickly returned her gaze to Robb. She entered his office and pulled the door shut behind her. The earlier smile evaporated. A worried frown occupied its former spot.

"What's the story behind St. Jerome Prep?"

Robb gave her a blank stare. Inwardly, her question stirred a much different reaction. His pulse quickened as he mulled over how he should answer her. Losing that job still stung. It had nothing to do with his job performance. Robb was a damn good teacher.

Then the Order of the Crimson Thorns stole that part of his life away from him — just like everything else.

"What do you mean?" he finally asked.

"You were terminated from your last school for inappropriate conduct." Lora scooted her glasses upward along the bridge of her nose. "Did you seriously believe I wouldn't find out?"

Fired for inappropriate conduct?

Robb scowled.

They really did a number on him. Not only was he not fired, but he was never in danger of being fired. His conduct with his students and other teachers was above reproach. He always kept his teaching duties separate from any business with The Order.

"That's a flat out lie!" Robb slammed his hands down on the edge of his desk. "You can't trust whoever made that claim to you. I left St. Jerome on good terms. Nobody booted me out the door."

He bit his tongue to avoid unloading the other things that popped into his head. No sense lighting a match and burning down this bridge. Staying in Deer Falls was non-negotiable until he gained the amulet's full power. If he packed up and relocated to a different town now, agents from The Order would have a much easier time tracking him down. He'd never stop running.

Robb needed to keep this job at all costs.

"Those reports I read tell a different story." A freshly cross tone threaded through Lora's voice. "Statements from students alleging verbal abuse. Video footage of you throwing markers across the room."

Robb's lips parted and he shook his head in disbelief. No incidents like the ones the principal described ever occurred inside his classroom. Someone framed him. End of story. No dark magic was necessary to complete the job either. Creating a deep-fake video and handing out a few bucks to persuade some greedy students to lie through their teeth would be sufficient.

"I swear none of those things happened," Robb insisted. "I give you my word. Don't believe what you've seen and read."

Lora crossed her arms and studied him carefully. She closed her eyelids for a moment and sighed.

"Can you provide evidence to the contrary?"

"I don't have anything with me." Robb cast a frantic glance down at his laptop screen. "But if you give me a little time, I —"

"You'll be placed on administrative leave pending a thorough review of the allegations by the school board," she said, interrupting him. "That's the best I can do under the circumstances."

His eyes trailed up to Lora again. She stared at him with a disapproving frown tattooed across her lips.

"I suggest you gather up your personal belongings and head home," Lora continued. "If I were you, I wouldn't count on coming back later.

She turned away from him and opened his office door again. Robb's eyes hardened and trailed Lora as she returned to her own office one door down in the short hall. How dare she do this to him? Forget about giving him a chance to defend himself against these allegations. This stupid ass small-town principal intended to kick him out of this high school as quickly as she let him in.

Robb instinctively pressed his palm against the amulet underneath his dress shirt. He glanced down at his chest. A wry smile formed on his lips. If Lora refused to be persuaded against firing him, this situation called for an alternative resolution.

He sprang to his feet and quietly opened the top drawer in his desk. Robb's fingers curled around a pair of scissors inside the drawer.

One of them would lose their job.

It wouldn't be him.

Robb stuck the scissors inside his back pocket. He marched down the hall and flung open the door to Lora's office. She nearly jumped out of her skin and cast eye daggers in his direction.

"What is the meaning of this?" Her icy tone mirrored her expression. "What do you think you're doing?"

"I've thought it over and decided against accepting administrative leave." Robb flashed a smirk at the principal. "I went to a lot of trouble to get this job and I'm not giving it up without a fight."

A crease formed in her brow.

"Are you threatening me?"

"Not at all." He stuck his hand behind his back. "This is me threatening you."

Robb drew out the scissors from his back pocket and brought them forward. He pointed them at the principal's face. Lora's eyes widened and she licked her lips.

"I'm calling the police."

Her threat produced a chuckle from Robb.

"They'll never make it here in time."

He followed her eyes as they slid over to the office door behind him. Robb uttered the same incantation which he used on Trace a few days earlier. At once, the door swung shut and the knob locked on its own. His smirk widened and he shook an index finger at Lora like a parent scolding an unruly child.

"You're not going anywhere."

She glanced over at the scissors. Fresh tears rolled down her cheeks.

"I'll give you what you want." She raised her hands, holding them suspended before her body like a makeshift shield. "Anything. I mean it. Promise you won't hurt me."

"Anything?" Robb repeated.

Lora rose from her chair. She pushed the front edge of the leather chair backward with her veiny calves.

"We can work this out." A palpable tremor seized her voice. "Please."

Witnessing Lora's growing terror amused and disgusted Robb in equal proportions. A tough-talking principal who lost her nerve when someone beat her at her own intimidation game. What a coward! She deserved her impending fate.

"Now we can work things out?" Robb's smile snapped into a deepening frown. "Do you only listen to other people when your life is on the line?"

Lora snatched a stapler from her desk and threw it at his head. The stapler struck his cheekbone. Robb's eyes narrowed and matched the rage reflected in his scowl. He charged toward the desk, scissors raised to ear level.

She scrambled across the top of her desk. Scattered papers and pens tumbled to the floor. Heavy breaths escaped from her lips, interspersed with continuous sobbing. Lora lost one shoe as she slid off the desk. It dropped to the floor beside her. Robb stopped at the side of the desk, pivoted, and changed direction.

The heel on her other shoe buckled as Lora tried to sprint for the exit. Her ankle rolled. She cried sharply and tumbled to the floor.

Robb pounced on the principal with the zeal of a cat who cornered a mouse. He tore her glasses from her face and flung them aside.

"No more fun and games," he sneered.

Robb grabbed Lora by her scalp, digging his fingers into her hair, and wrenched her neck backward. With his other hand, he plunged the scissors through her right eye. Blood spurted out around the blades and dribbled down her cheek.

Lora let out a sudden gasp and fell silent.

He drew out the amulet from under his shirt and pressed it against her forehead. Fresh gleaming energy streamed from Lora's dying body into his own. Robb's tongue passed over his lips and he pressed his eyelids shut as he drank in this new surge of power.

Nothing else equaled the exhilaration.

15

Crime scene photos occupied most of the laptop screen. Leeds planted his elbows on his oak desk and rested his chin on interlocked fingers. He studied the strange symbol burned in the foreheads of both victims from last month's double homicide on Silvertooth Road. Testing on collected DNA samples proved inconclusive. Whoever murdered Angelique Woods and Troy McCord did an excellent job of covering their tracks after the fact.

Nothing outside of that lone symbol offered a clue to the unsub's actual identity.

"This is going nowhere." Leeds let out a frustrated sigh. "There's a connection here. I know it. I gotta find it."

The mysterious reaper amulet formed a connecting thread between all three recent homicides. Devouring flames left only charred remnants of Trace Fowler's corpse wedged inside a burnt-out shell of a mangled car. Still, the forensics team found a faint imprint on the slain teen's skull matching a symbol found on the other two bodies. Discovering the same unusual symbol at two otherwise unconnected crime scenes showed an unmistakable signature of a serial killer.

Leeds leaned back in his chair, folded his arms, and pursed his lips. Heavy eyes drifted over to an empty navy-blue mug on his desk. Another coffee refill called to him from the break room.

"It's gonna be another long night," he mumbled.

Leeds pushed off from the arms of his chair and rose to his feet. Coffee offered the promise of a fresh jolt of energy, but it lacked the ability to clear his head. These cases required examination from a fresh angle through a different lens.

"10-54d. Possible 187. At the high school."

His heart sank when Leeds heard the code shared on his police radio. Not again. Not another murder victim.

Leeds pressed the talk button on his radio.

"On my way. ETA 10 minutes."

A heavy sigh escaped his lips as he departed from the sheriff's office and headed out to his cruiser. This job started to gnaw at him more than usual. Leeds put so much daily energy into trying to make Deer Falls a safe place to live. Moments like these ones made him feel like a complete failure.

Long conversations with Mariah often led to longer debates over leaving Deer Falls and taking a job in a different safer town. Leeds learned his wife didn't see eye-to-eye with him on this decision. Gruesome fates that befell Palmer and other past deputies did not sway her into agreeing to pack all their belongings into a moving truck and restart their family's life in a new place.

"This is our home," Mariah said when he last broached the topic with her back in June. "Our friends and our children's friends are all here. You're asking us to sacrifice the lives we built in Deer Falls and start from scratch."

Leeds recalled how he rose from the kitchen table and turned his face toward a sliding door leading into the backyard. He peered through smudged glass while trying to conceal growing frustration from Mariah. His eyes settled on a long and narrow flower box. Rows of sunflowers and daisies in full bloom climbed from the shady box and stretched toward the sun. Those flowers served as a fitting symbol for their family. Autumn cuts short the life of each flower. Leeds feared living in Deer Falls for much longer would bring a similar fate upon him, Mariah, and their children.

'I know I'm asking a difficult thing from you." Leeds finally turned back to the table and sought eye contact with his wife again. "I want our family to feel happy. But I also want us to be safe. I just don't believe that's possible any longer here in Deer Falls."

"Where do you want us to go?"

"What do you mean?"

"Where can we go that will guarantee us permanent safety, Jackson?" Mariah asked. "No utopia exists where we can hide from the rest of the world."

Her words from a few months ago lingered with Leeds on his drive over to a fresh crime scene at the high school. Mariah wasn't wrong to be skeptical. Assuming life would turn out safer or less complicated elsewhere amounted to naive thinking. Deer Falls couldn't be the only living magnet for unholy supernatural entities.

Leeds pulled his cruiser into the bus lane and parked in front of the high school. He shut off the vehicle's siren. Only traces of sunlight lingered on the horizon. The sun had long since retreated behind the mountains for the night. Leeds bowed his head, crossed himself, and opened his door.

Dread seeped into his body and spread out from head to toe with every step he took from his cruiser to the high school's main entrance. Leeds mentally prepared himself for the worst. Nothing he silently told himself eased the shock from witnessing the gruesome scene preserved before his eyes.

Lora Reynolds, the high school principal, lay sprawled in a shallow drying pool of blood between her desk and office door. A pair of scissors stuck out of the socket Lora's right eye once occupied alone. She bore the same symbol from the reaper amulet in her forehead.

Unmistakable evidence a serial killer was terrorizing their town.

Leeds ducked under the yellow crime scene tape and entered the office. Loose papers and a stapler were scattered across the floor near the body. Signs of a struggle. He crouched down before the corpse after their crime scene photographer snapped one last photo. Leeds studied the principal's lifeless face frozen in an expression of shocked agony. What sick bastard was doing this? Why did the unsub target her? Why did they target any of the people they targeted?

No obvious connections between the four victims were clear beyond the same haunting symbol.

"Do we have any witnesses?"

Leeds straightened his legs and rose to a standing position again as he posed the question. He cast his eyes toward Greer — his deputy who first arrived on scene. She frowned and shook her head.

"Nobody we talked to saw or heard what happened," Greer said. "A custodian stumbled upon the body near the end of his shift."

"He didn't notice anything unusual before that?"

"Well, the custodian told me he ran a floor waxer in the gym for a half hour or so. Couldn't hear anything over the noise."

"Damn."

"I know. Only found the body because he noticed a light on inside her office while returning the waxer to a custodial closet."

"Does he know if anyone else was working late at the school besides Principal Reynolds?"

Greer rubbed an open palm along the side of her neck, her fingers brushing against a blonde ponytail, and shook her head again.

"I tracked down the staff list," she said. "Lots of teachers and aides to comb through. We'll have to interview them all. See if we turn up a solid suspect."

"That's a good …"

Leeds trailed off and paused. He raised his index finger and snapped his head toward the open door. A muffled conversation emanating from the hallway greeted his ears. Leeds ducked under crime scene tape again and popped outside the doorway. Two figures, partially shrouded in shadow, stood in a hall leading from the principal's office to a set of classrooms on the south end of the school building.

One figure Leeds identified as the custodian whom Greer interviewed earlier. The other one skulking by the lockers he did not recognize.

"Can I ask what you're doing here?" Leeds called out. "This is a crime scene. You're interfering with an active investigation."

The gray-haired custodian jerked his head toward him. His wrinkled eyes widened. He pointed at himself with some hesitation.

Leeds shook his head.

"No, Elmer, you're free to go," he said. "But I want your friend over there to stick around for a bit. Got some questions I'd like to ask."

Relief instantly washed over the custodian's face. Elmer nodded and excused himself. The other person stepped out of the shadowy hall and approached Leeds. Her pale green eyes clashed with raven hair and equally dark lipstick.

"You don't need to worry about me, Sheriff." She spoke in a soft tone. Her words carried a hint of a southern drawl. "The name is Amy Boyle. I'm a private investigator based out of Denver."

Amy extended her hand. A tattoo circling her wrist peeked out from under her jacket sleeve. The image resembled blood-tinged thorns fashioned into a crown. Leeds cast a wary eye at the private eye and decided against shaking her hand.

"Can you show me your PI license?"

She flashed an earnest smile and pointed to a black purse hanging at her side.

"I have it inside my wallet. I'd be happy to bring it out for you."

Leeds nodded. Amy plunged her hand inside the purse and drew out a matching wallet a second later. She cracked open the wallet and handed a laminated card to him. He studied the card for a moment. Amy's claim checked out. The license was genuine and current.

"What are you doing at my crime scene?" he asked, handing the license back to her. "I didn't ask for a private eye. I didn't authorize my deputies to hire one either."

"I'm consulting with the Denver PD on a case," she said. "Sent me to Deer Falls to chase a lead."

Leeds crossed his arms.

"What lead? What case?"

Amy jammed her license and her wallet back inside her purse. Her smile vanished when she made eye contact with him again.

"What exactly do you know about Robb Cooper?"

He shrugged.

"Not much beyond superficial details. Moved to Deer Falls a while ago." Leeds glanced over his shoulder at the principal's office and back at her. "He's the new assistant principal here at the high school."

"Cooper is a person of interest in an unsolved murder case back in Denver." Amy drew out a smartphone from her purse this time. "He skipped town before anyone brought him in for questioning."

She swiped the screen multiple times and finally handed the phone over to Leeds. The screen displayed a recent *Denver Post* article detailing the slaying of Ethan Garvey. Leeds recalled seeing a brief report of his homicide on the local news. Local investigators suspected Garvey had been murdered in the aftermath of a drug deal gone wrong.

No one from the Denver police ever contacted him about the assistant principal. As he scrolled through the article, a distinct thought struck Leeds. This current string of gruesome murders occurred after Robb Cooper arrived in town.

Timing between those events stood out as more than a mere coincidence. Cooper presented a solid alibi when Leeds questioned him earlier over what happened to the Fowler boy. Serious doubts about that alibi now surfaced in his mind.

"I appreciate the information," he said, handing the phone back to Amy. "Now I suggest you head back to Denver. Let me and my deputies handle Cooper on our own terms."

Her frown deepened.

"That's a bad idea. I don't think you fully grasp how dangerous this man is. You need my help."

Leeds flashed a brief smirk and chuckled at her brashness. Ask a private eye for help?

Not a chance.

"I'll be sure to reach out to the Denver PD if I need their help," he replied. "Now do I need to help you find your car?"

She raised her hands and backed away.

"I'm leaving."

Leeds kept his eyes cemented on Amy as she turned away from him. His gaze never strayed from the private eye until she pushed open one of the double doors serving as the school's main entrance and walked through to the other side. Private investigators did not number among his favorite people. Ones whom he dealt with in the past used far too many unscrupulous methods to obtain crucial information. Still, running into Amy offered Leeds a promising new break in these murder cases.

Digging deeper to uncover the truth meant paying their new assistant principal a second visit.

Eric nearly collided with his mom when he dashed into the kitchen. She slid her feet out of his path at the last second and braced her hand against the edge of the kitchen island. Emily tilted her head and flashed a crooked smile which only partially concealed the annoyance bubbling behind her eyes.

"Where's the fire?" she asked. "We have a speed limit inside this house, you know."

Eric's hand, with fingers securely clamped on his smartphone, dropped to his side. He stopped in front of the refrigerator and wheeled around. Eric glanced over at her and offered an apologetic shrug.

"Sorry. Max and Tatiana just texted me. We're gonna go chill since classes are canceled today."

Emily nodded and ran her teeth across her bottom lip.

"That school is a mess again," she said. "Two violent deaths only a few days apart."

Eric said nothing, only drawing a sharp breath. News of the grisly fate that befell Principal Reynolds reached them earlier that morning. The Deer Falls School District superintendent sent an email saying classes would be canceled for the remainder of the week. Learning about the principal's murder wreaked extra havoc on Eric's already fragile nerves.

First Trace.

16

Now her.

He couldn't help looking over his shoulder more frequently than before. An unseen adversary seemed to be toying with him. Both deaths happened to people connected to Eric in a specific way.

Was he next?

Or his family and friends?

"I need to clear my mind," he said. "Spending a few hours with my friends might do the trick."

"Sounds like we both have plans."

Eric arched an eyebrow and mirrored his mom's earlier head tilt.

"What plans?"

"Nothing too big. Just a little date."

Emily's enthusiastic tone and wide grin betrayed her efforts to downplay her plans. Her reaction raised Eric's suspicions. The note she left the other day re-entered his mind. Two dates within a few days — that he knew of.

"Do you have a boyfriend?"

Eric posed the question while feeling uncertain he wanted to know the answer. Dating hadn't been a serious pursuit for her since they moved to Deer Falls. Emily claimed repeatedly she had sworn off men since the divorce.

Such a resolution suited Eric just fine. His dad ended up being a total asshole in the end. No need for his mom to risk bringing another unsavory dude cut from the same cloth into their lives.

"I ... don't know." Emily hesitated and looked away. She trailed her index finger in a tight circle on the countertop. "There's some potential. Definite ... sparks."

He groaned internally. His mom's body language told him exactly what he needed to know. Eric's fears were coming true before his eyes. All signs pointed to an unwanted boyfriend in the making.

"Who's the guy?"

Joy threaded through her eyes as she glanced back at him. Emily dug her phone out of her pocket and swiped the screen. She clicked an app icon and retrieved a photo before passing the phone over to him.

The photo showed her taking a selfie with a brown-haired man in front of the Silver Fork Diner. Eric instantly recognized him.

His face fell.

"You're dating my assistant principal?"

"Robb is your assistant principal?" His mom's expression matched the surprise laced through her voice. "He told me he was a teacher, but I thought he worked at the junior high. Must have misheard him."

"This isn't good." Eric shook his head and handed the phone back. "Not good at all."

Emily knit her brows together and studied his face. Her not-so-subtle attempt to read him and perceive his thoughts made Eric feel like a human version of one of her edited manuscripts she scoured for elusive typos. His mom's face relaxed again a moment later and her smile returned.

"You worry too much," Emily said. "I'll bet money he won't turn out like the others."

"You're making a big assumption," Eric said. "You barely know him."

"Nah. He's such a sweet and charming man." Her eyes settled on the selfie she took with Robb earlier. "Plus, he's easy on the eyes."

Eric scrunched up his face and shuddered.

"You've got the hots for my assistant principal? Good God. This won't end well for either of us."

Emily flashed a perturbed frown at him.

"Don't let me keep you from hanging out with your friends."

Her blunt tone and subsequent dismissive wave told Eric he crossed a line he probably shouldn't have crossed. Knowledge of a disturbing potential coupling between his mom and the assistant principal burrowed into his thoughts long after he left the kitchen. Eric almost forgot to grab his toboggan after he bundled up in a dark blue coat, knitted cap, and boots before heading out the door.

Max, Tatiana, and Devin all met up with him inside the arched entryway to the town park. They trudged across hardened snow toward a hill on the opposite side of a frozen duck pond. The hill was set back 40 yards from a paved walking trail winding around the teardrop-shaped pond's perimeter. Eric cradled his toboggan between his ribs and left elbow as he climbed the hill, matching the eager strides of his friends. All three carried their own sleds.

"I don't care what kind of sled you've got, you still can't outrace me," Tatiana said, casting a sideways glance at Devin. "That's the truth."

Devin answered with a confident smile.

"Not my truth." He stuck his inflatable bullet sled out in front of him like a shield. "Alex told me nothing else can touch this sled's top speed."

She rolled her eyes and snickered at his claim.

"No offense, Devin," Tatiana scoffed. "But your brother has smoked one too many joints for me to trust anything he says."

Devin's smile snapped into a frown. He planted his sled down on the snow when they reached the hilltop and pointed the sled's nose back at the steep slope. Tatiana adjusted the faded green knit cap covering her ears and mirrored his actions.

"Your turn to put up or shut up," Devin said.

Neither teen waited for Eric or Max to drop their sleds before they shot down the hill. Max let loose a loud laugh when Devin zipped past Tatiana and reached the bottom first. She climbed off her belly, turned, and shot an icy glare back up the slope.

"Best two out of three," Tatiana said.

"Prepare to be last out of four," Max shouted.

He mimed pulling back the string on a bow and releasing an arrow. Tatiana flipped him off. Max laughed again, dropped his sled on the snow ahead of him, and flopped belly first on top. Eric set his toboggan down on a parallel spot. Both teens pushed off from the packed snow with a steering foot and their sleds coasted down the steep slope. Each one picked up increased speed as it succumbed to gravity's whims.

White powder sprayed skyward on either side as Eric's toboggan journeyed toward the bottom. His trajectory sent the toboggan on a curving path toward a cluster of trees bordering the west side of the hill. Eric drew a sharp breath and quickly jerked the front of the toboggan upward. Once it slowed a bit, he planted his right foot in the snow to steer away from trees.

He let out a relieved sigh when the terrain leveled out again at the bottom of the hill. Eric planted his other foot in the snow to force a full stop.

"Dude, I beat you like a drum." Max greeted him with a laugh while springing off his sled a few feet ahead of Eric's toboggan. "Why did you slow up midway down the hill? We've made this run tons of times."

Eric shrugged and rose to his feet.

"Don't know. I started veering toward those trees." He pointed over at the west side of the hill. "When I saw where I was going, I got a bad vibe."

"Bad vibe?" Max repeated.

Eric rubbed his hands over his cheeks. He started feeling like equal parts dork and fool for saying anything.

"I'm fine. Forget I said anything."

"Are you?"

"Let's climb the hill and take another crack. Best two out of three. Like Tatiana said."

Max folded his arms and eyed him suspiciously. Eric glanced away from him and rested his gaze on Tatiana and Devin. They had walked away from their sleds to join them and now mirrored Max's body language.

"This is gonna sound stupid, but my mom is dating again. It's got me off balance."

Tatiana instantly lit up with a curious smile.

"Give us the 411. Who's she dating?"

Eric pinched his lips together into a worried frown.

"The new assistant principal."

Devin let out a spontaneous laugh. Tatiana scrunched up her eyes and nose and shook her head.

"Gross. Some lines shouldn't be crossed."

"Mom didn't see it that way. She told me he's 'easy on the eyes.' She's so blind."

Eric emphasized Emily's description of Robb Cooper with air quotes. Max made a silent gagging motion. Devin puckered his lips and pinched his eyelids shut. Eric shot him a cross stare.

"That's all sorts of disturbing," Tatiana said.

"We should go on one of those websites where you can do a background check on someone," Max replied. "Find out if he's got anything to hide. You can dig up anything on those sites."

Eric's frown snapped into a smile and an approving nod followed.

"Bet."

The foursome packed up their sleds and traveled over to Eric's house. Eric suggested his home as their destination because he suspected Cooper would arrive later to pick up his mom. Being at the house when Cooper showed up offered a chance for him to watch how this dude interacted with his mom and see if any red flags jumped out.

No unfamiliar vehicles were parked in the driveway or along the curb when Eric made it home. After his friends arrived, he led them up the porch steps, unlocked the front door and pushed it open.

"Mom," Eric called out. "Are you home?"

Nothing except sounds of running water greeted him inside. Eric cocked his head toward the stairs. The shower ran at full blast behind a locked bathroom door.

"We're on the final countdown for your mom's date," Devin said, cracking a grin.

Eric gave him a side-eye glance but said nothing. He motioned to the others to follow him.

"My laptop is in my bedroom upstairs."

Lyrics to a happy song greeted Eric when he reached the landing. He cast an immediate anxious glance at the bathroom door. Tatiana snickered behind him.

"I just love your mom," she said.

Why did his mom pick now of all times to bust out a song in the shower? Eric wanted to crawl deep under a rock and hide until her private concert-for-one stopped. Sure, she had a good voice. Still, her talent didn't make this moment feel any less embarrassing.

He quickly ushered Max, Devin, and Tatiana into his bedroom and shut the door. Eric walked over to a desk in the corner, dropped down into the chair, and powered up his laptop. An open browser window, displaying a search engine page, popped up on the screen after the computer finished booting.

"Google 'Rob Cooper principal.'"

Eric rolled his eyes and shook his head. Devin's suggestion wasn't remotely helpful.

"That'll bring up a million results," he said without bothering to look back at him. "I think —"

"We should search for 'Rob Cooper criminal record' first," Tatiana blurted out. "You can do a background check on a ton of different sites."

She leaned over Eric's shoulder like she intended to slide her hands over the keyboard and enter the search term herself. A distinct creamy vanilla aroma tickled his nose. Did Tatiana stop and put on perfume before coming over to his house? She smelled so good. And the way her amber brown locks teasingly dangled down her cheeks from underneath her ski cap …

Eric drew a sharp breath and forcefully blinked a couple of times. This is Tatiana. She's a friend. They had been friends since freshman year. He didn't want to ruin their friendship. Eric forced himself to refocus his attention on the laptop screen.

Following Tatiana's suggestion brought no promising new information. Two different men named Rob Cooper appeared in the search results. One lived in Florida, the other in Iowa. Neither one bore resemblance to their assistant principal.

"I'm telling you — Rob Cooper principal," Devin insisted. "Just type those words in. Trust me. My gut says this is the way."

Eric typed *Rob Cooper teacher* into the search engine instead. Search results produced a staff directory listing for a school called St. Jerome Prep Academy in Denver. An accompanying photo confirmed this was indeed their assistant principal.

"He spells Robb with a second b?" Tatiana said, letting out an incredulous sigh. "Dude is odd. Your mom shouldn't ship with him for that reason alone."

"Facts," Eric replied.

He clicked on the staff directory link. Cooper's staff page had been removed and the link now redirected back to the school's home page. Eric doubled back and retrieved an archived version from the previous school year. The old staff page revealed a tantalizing fact.

Robb Cooper was married.

His wife's name was Amy.

"Married?" Anger rose in Eric's voice. "What the hell? Is he trying to catfish my mom?"

"Bro, you gotta warn her," Max said. "Last thing your mom needs is a slimy married dude trying to hook up with her."

Damn straight he had to warn her. Quickly. Why didn't his mom check this stuff out before deciding to date this loser?

A ringing doorbell pierced through Eric's thoughts.

"That's him!"

He sprang out of his chair and raced out of the bedroom. The other three teens followed hot on Eric's heels down the hall. Eric had a small window. If he caught Emily before she left, then he could share these revelations with her and put an immediate end to Cooper's charade.

His mom opened the front door when Eric was only halfway down the stairs. Cooper greeted her with a warm embrace and a peck on the lips after the door closed behind him. Eric froze and shuddered.

A married man kissed his mom.

The assistant principal glanced toward the stairs when he pulled back again. Surprise and recognition filled his eyes as they settled on Eric. He stared at him briefly before his gaze shifted back to Emily.

Cooper cracked a wry smile.

"You didn't tell me you had a younger brother."

She answered him with a broad grin and gave his shoulder a playful slap with the back of her hand.

"Stop! Eric is my baby boy. I already told you I had one teen and one recent college graduate."

"You're messing with me. No way you're old enough to be a mom to a teenager."

Cooper's inane attempts at flattery made Eric want to barf almost as much as watching him kiss his mom earlier. His eyes darted down to the assistant principal's hands. No wedding band circled either ring finger. One crucial detail in his careful deception. That tool had no business spending time with her or being in this house.

"Did you used to sweet talk Amy the same way as you're doing with my mom?" Eric asked.

A confused frown instantly forced the smile off Cooper's face. He backpedaled a couple of steps and answered him with a probing stare. Emily glanced briefly over her shoulder at Eric and quickly returned her gaze to the assistant principal.

"Who's Amy?" she asked, eyeing him with suspicion.

An uncomfortable silence settled like a thick haze over the room. Eric glared at Cooper, refusing to break eye contact. His mom needed to know the truth. She didn't deserve to be strung along by another jerk concealing ulterior motives.

"I didn't want you to find out like this," Cooper finally said, piercing the silence. "Amy is my ex-wife."

"Ex-wife?"

"Yeah. Our divorce was finalized a year ago. This is the first time I've felt comfortable dating again."

Emily glanced down at his naked ring finger. She flashed a sympathetic smile.

"I know too well how that goes," Emily said. "Seven years have elapsed since mine."

Cooper's smile returned. He stepped forward again and clasped her arm just above her elbow.

"Well, he's a grade F fool."

This did not go down the way Eric envisioned. He stole a glance at his friends standing on the stairs above him and scowled. Max only shrugged. Tatiana and Devin said nothing.

"You have a beautiful ring," Cooper said. "What gemstone is that?"

"Garnet." Emily fidgeted with the ring. "It's my birthstone."

"Can I see it?"

She nodded and slid it off her finger. The ring spilled out of her fingertips when she extended her hand and clattered against the floor.

"Let me get that for you."

Cooper dropped to his knees and leaned over to snatch up the fallen ring. An unusual looking amulet popped out from under his button-up collared shirt. Eric's eyes were drawn to the jewelry.

It resembled twin scythe blades forming a cross.

His throat tightened and his heartbeat quickened. That amulet matched the hand-drawn image Sheriff Leeds showed him and his mom when he questioned Eric about Trace's death.

He instantly averted his gaze when Cooper rose to his feet again. When Eric's eyes trailed back over to the assistant principal, the amulet had been tucked back into its original spot underneath his shirt.

Cooper's eyes drilled down into him.

"Got any fun plans for tonight?"

Eric tried to play it cool, pretending he never noticed anything out of the ordinary. His nerves didn't want to cooperate.

"Um … you know … Netflix and …"

"Chill?"

Eric nodded and licked his lips.

"Something like that."

His mom flashed a disapproving frown at him.

"You know my rules about having girls over here."

Eric turned and glanced back up the stairs at Tatiana. Her confused expression mirrored his own.

"Besides Tatiana," Emily added.

Uncomfortable silence paid a second visit. Eric wondered if his mom also caught a glimpse of the amulet. If she did, she mastered the art of playing coy about this startling revelation.

"We probably ought to head out," his mom finally said. "Stay out of trouble while we're gone."

Eric worried less about getting himself into trouble than he did for her safety. Cooper bore responsibility for Trace's death. Did he also kill the principal? This new evidence pointed to one disturbing fact.

His mom was dating a cold-blooded murderer.

17

Handmade pottery adorned a series of staggered white wooden boxes stacked across the laminate floor. Emily snatched up a ceramic pitcher from its perch and studied intricate patterns crisscrossing the glazed surface from top to bottom. A relaxed smile crept over her lips while she admired the artistic flair and craftsmanship.

"I told you this alone was worth a trek to Golden."

She glanced up at Robb and nodded. Emily wished Deer Falls had a holiday art market like the one here in the art center. Even a small local gallery would be a nice addition and go a long way to making the little mountain town feel less like a cultural wasteland.

Having closer proximity to art probably wouldn't serve her monthly budget well. Emily piled up quite a large collection when she still lived in Commerce City. Turning around and selling off several pieces later following her divorce was painful but proved necessary.

Their moving truck simply did not have enough space to transport everything she wanted to keep.

"I love this place," Emily said. "I could spend an entire day in here and not get bored."

Robb cracked a grin.

"Feel free to pick out some pottery to take home," he said. "My treat."

Her smile widened. She set down the pitcher again and threw her arms around him in a warm embrace.

"You are the best. How did I ever find you?"

Robb cast his eyes skyward for a moment and then looked back at Emily thoughtfully while holding her inside his arms.

"Fate. Luck. Whatever you want to call it, I think it's worked out well for us."

"Indeed."

She planted an impromptu kiss on his lips and then pulled back from the embrace. Emily scooped up a matching pitcher and vase from a nearby box. Their sandstone coloring alone made them aesthetically appealing. She and Robb wound their way past the other artistic wares to a cash register. Emily set both items on the counter as he drew out a credit card from his wallet.

An odd feeling gripped her as an art center employee rang up the purchase. Emily turned and gazed at the pottery display again. A raven-haired woman in a black coat stood near the end of the outermost box. Mirrored sunglasses covered her eyes, but she was quite obviously staring at Robb and Emily herself.

Why? Did she also want to buy the sandstone pottery Emily picked out earlier?

The raven-haired woman averted her eyes as soon as she noticed Emily returning her stare. She picked up a ceramic bowl and studied it intently. Emily furrowed her brow and returned her gaze to Robb.

"Is something wrong?" he asked.

"A woman with mirrored sunglasses was standing over by the pottery and staring at us," she said.

Robb glanced over at the same spot and shrugged.

"I don't see her now. She must have left."

Emily peeked over her shoulder and confirmed the woman had disappeared.

"Huh. Maybe she wanted the pitcher and vase I picked out."

"Too bad for her." Robb gathered up the sack holding Emily's new pottery and handed it to her. "First come, first serve."

They walked out of the art center and returned to his sedan. Robb clicked his fob and opened the passenger door. Emily dropped down into the seat and set the pottery between her feet, along with her purse, while she latched her seatbelt. He closed the door and rounded the car's front end.

When Emily scooped up the pottery-filled sack into her arms again, she caught a glimpse of the same raven-haired woman from earlier. She stood outside the art center's main door and leaned against a handrail near the top of the winding stairs. Icy wisps escaped from her lips as she stared straight ahead at the sedan.

"Look!" Emily tapped Robb on the shoulder with the back of her hand. "Do you see that?"

He lifted his chin and glanced over at her.

"See what?"

"Over there." She pointed toward the art center door. "That woman's back. She's staring ..."

Emily trailed off when she realized the woman in the black coat vanished a second time. Robb gave her a quizzical look as he started the engine.

"I think you're worried about nothing."

She rubbed her hands over her cheeks and frowned. Emily didn't like the implication she was being paranoid.

"I'm not imagining things. That woman seems to be following us — or me, at least."

"It's probably just a coincidence. Don't let her ruin our night."

Sound advice from Robb. Still, Emily couldn't help staring at the stairs and door as the sedan pulled away from the curb and traveled down Washington Avenue. The woman's presence left her with an unsettling vibe. Her persistence in watching them felt more personal than being miffed at not obtaining her pottery of choice first.

"So, I finally checked out your book," Robb said.

Emily snapped her head back to him and cracked a knowing smile.

"Which one? I've published several."

"You know which one. The same book that everyone and their dog talks about."

Yeah, Emily knew exactly which novel he referenced. These days, everyone seemingly read or claimed they read *The Witching Hour* and nothing else. Emily enjoyed earning widespread recognition for her hard work at last, but she also feared gaining a reputation for being a one-hit wonder as an author.

"Where did you get your inspiration?" Robb continued. "The story and characters felt so real, almost like you drew on personal experiences."

A hesitant smile crossed her lips. If only Emily had the freedom to share the complete story with him. She wanted to tell Robb everything that happened during her ordeal with Cassandra. Emily resisted giving into that urge. She didn't want to ruin their nascent relationship.

Few people were ready to accept the notion that magic was both real and dangerous. If Robb was a skeptic of the supernatural, he'd likely dismiss her experiences out of hand. Emily wouldn't accept them herself if she hadn't lived through them first. She didn't feel ready to face the sting of rejection. Keeping this secret was tough but necessary.

The timing for a revelation didn't feel right. Yet.

"Deer Falls has a ton of fascinating urban legends," she said. "You don't have to travel very far to find inspiration for a scary story."

"That's convenient," Robb replied, adding a chuckle. "Saves you on airline miles."

They traveled north toward the Golden Freeway. Robb clicked on his headlights when the sun dipped below the horizon. Two headlights belonging to a car right behind his sedan clicked on at the same time.

Emily barely took note of the other car until she observed peculiar behavior from the other driver. Whenever Robb changed lanes, the trailing vehicle mimicked his action and tried to keep pace with the sedan. Even when he entered the freeway, those same headlights lingered as a fixed presence in their back window.

Were they being followed?

Robb noticed the other vehicle too. He narrowed his eyes and glanced up at his rearview mirror.

"Is it me or has the same car been behind us since we drove away from the art center?" he asked.

Emily licked her lips and glanced at the passenger side mirror. It warned that objects in the mirror were closer than they appeared. This specific object stayed too close for comfort for too long.

"Someone is definitely following us." Her widening eyes slid over to Robb. "This is freaking me out."

"Let's not panic. We can test our theory out."

"How?"

"I'll find an exit and we'll make four consecutive right turns. If they make the same turns, then it will confirm our suspicions."

"What do we do if that happens?"

Robb's eyes skated over to Emily. A resolute frown washed over him.

"Simple. We lose them ourselves or we find help."

She snapped her head back to the passenger side mirror. Robb searched for a freeway exit and barreled down the exit ramp when they finally reached one. The other car kept up its pursuit. Four right turns on four different streets brought no change.

Their pursuer stuck to Robb's sedan like glue.

"My God," he said. "This is one persistent jerk."

"Let's find a police station," Emily said. She struggled to peel her eyes away from the mirror while the other car continued its pursuit. "They won't follow us there."

An uncomfortable pause greeted her suggestion. Emily glanced over at Robb. Worry swam through his eyes and his arms grew rigid as he gripped the steering wheel. She scrunched up her face. Robb's body language hinted at a major apprehension toward involving the local police in their predicament.

"What do you suggest we do?" Emily asked.

"Keep your eyes on the other car." Robb glanced over at her. "Tell me when we've lost them."

She forced a smile and focused her attention on the passenger side mirror again. An ethereal beam flashed across her peripheral vision. Ashen mist billowed up from the pavement between Robb's sedan and the pursuing car. It formed a milky wall across the road, obscuring the other vehicle from her sight.

Screeching brakes and a crash punctured the mist in a sudden, violent cacophony. Emily's lips trembled as the sounds of crunching metal and shattering glass reached her inside the car. Did the mist harden into an actual solid wall? Only one plausible answer lay before her, an explanation she dared not speak aloud.

Dark magic caused this.

Emily looked over at Robb. He stared unblinking at the road before them. One hand rested on the steering wheel. The other clutched a fistful of fabric from his button-up shirt.

"What just happened back there? Where did that mist come from?"

She played dumb with her questions, not wanting to clue him into her past encounters with magic. How would he react if he learned the truth? Robb finally blinked and relaxed his hand, letting it drop from his shirt. He glanced over at Emily and shrugged.

"Your guess is as good as mine."

A crease formed in her brow, but she said nothing. Her thoughts were not silenced. Robb's oblivious reaction to the mist didn't add up. What exactly was he doing with his hand when she looked over at him?

Silence reigned inside the sedan while Emily puzzled over what unfolded. They reached the freeway again when a new pair of lights appeared behind their car.

Flashing red and blue lights.

Their sudden appearance wrenched Emily out of her troubled thoughts. She snapped her head back to Robb again. His eyes darted over to the rearview mirror.

"Were you speeding?"

"I didn't do anything wrong." A palpable nervousness laced through his voice. "What do they want?"

"You better pull over and find out."

A defeated frown sprouted on his face. Robb clicked on his turn signal at the entrance ramp and guided his sedan across the white line over to the shoulder. He shifted it into the park and planted his forehead against the steering wheel. Visible frustration threaded through every line in his face.

Emily drew a deep breath and exhaled slowly, trying to calm her rattled nerves. She turned to Robb and tried to offer a reassuring smile.

"Stay calm. I'm sure it's no big deal. Maybe your taillight is out."

Robb raised his head. A visible imprint of the steering wheel remained on his forehead. He rubbed his hands over his eyes and down his cheeks, punctuating the motion with a sigh.

"Let's pray you're right."

Robb rolled down his window as a Colorado State Patrol trooper exited the cruiser behind them and approached the sedan. The trooper's nonchalant gait did not ease Emily's nerves. A flashlight beam fell on their faces when he reached the open window. She squinted and quickly shielded her eyes with her forearm.

"Do you know why I pulled you over?"

Robb shrugged.

"I'm sorry. I'm not certain to be honest. Was I speeding? Is my taillight out?"

The trooper answered neither question.

"License, registration, and proof of insurance, please."

"My license and insurance card are in my wallet inside my coat pocket." Robb glided his hand inside his coat as he spoke. "Can you tell me what's wrong?"

He cracked open the wallet and drew out both his license and insurance card. Robb glanced at Emily and motioned to the glove compartment with his head.

"Can you grab my registration?"

Emily nodded and yanked the compartment door open. She fished through a pile of old gas receipts and drew out the registration. Robb handed both requested items to the trooper. He flipped the flashlight beam over to Robb's driver's license and walked back to his cruiser. When the trooper returned to the sedan again, his deepening scowl told an unwelcome story.

"Step out of the vehicle, sir."

Robb unleashed a brief irritated sigh, unlatched his seat belt, and opened the driver's side door. Emily's heart pounded harder and faster. Her instincts told her this was more than a routine traffic stop. The trooper directed Robb to the back of his sedan. Emily unlatched her seatbelt and leaned over the cup holders. She concentrated on the rearview mirror, trying to catch a glimpse of everything going on behind her.

The trooper whipped out a pistol without warning and ordered Robb to put his hands behind his head. Robb stopped and stiffened in one spot like a tree trunk. He stood, unmoving, between two bumpers. A fierce look permeated his eyes, matching his resolute frown. An anxious sigh escaped from deep inside her.

This was fast turning into a date from hell.

What are you doing? Emily thought. *Let the cop give you a damn speeding ticket so we can go home.*

Blinding light sprang forth from the cruiser's headlights, simultaneously swallowing the trooper and Robb whole. It flooded every inch of pavement between both vehicles. Even after turning her head away, intense beams beat down on Emily and she squinted.

Two gunshots rang out amid bright light.

Terrified screams sliced through the icy winter air. Violent screams a person unleashes before death stakes a final claim. Both headlight beams ebbed back to their normal intensity. Emily quickly refocused her gaze on the rearview mirror.

She gasped.

Robb crouched over the trembling trooper, pressing an amulet against his forehead. An eerie purplish light climbed from the fallen trooper up through his arm. It spread across Robb's neck and face, illuminating individual veins like a string of lights on a Christmas tree. He pinched his eyelids shut and heaved his chest and arms as though experiencing pure ecstasy.

The trooper stopped twitching and his head slumped against the ground. Blood dripped from his open lips on the pavement. Glassy eyes cast a vacant stare at the sedan's back wheel.

Emily's lips trembled as she pressed her hand against her mouth. Tears rolled unbidden down her cheeks. Eric was right to be suspicious of Robb, even though it was for a completely different reason. She should have given more serious weight to her son's misgivings.

Robb wielded dark magic.

Exactly like Cassandra before him.

Emily leaned back against her seat and buried her face in both hands. Oh God. Did he intend to do to her what he did to the cop who pulled them over?

She opened her purse and fished around for her smartphone. Emily's instincts drove her to call for help. Who? Who in the world could save her out here in Golden? Deer Falls was too far away for Eric to reach her in time. Christina and Ron had moved out to Utah.

"What are you doing?"

Emily nearly jumped out of her skin upon hearing his voice again. A distinct sharpness infused Robb's question. Her smartphone fell from her hand and dropped back inside the purse.

"Who are … you?" she stammered. "What … are you?"

Disappointment threaded through Robb's face as his eyes fell on her tear-stained cheeks. He dipped his chin to his chest and sighed.

"Such a lovely date." He raised his head and met her eyes again. "Believed you were the one. I'd grown so lonely after losing Amy. Then that damn lackey from The Order refused to leave us in peace."

The Order.

Robb practically spat those two words out of his mouth. Emily had no clue who or what he referenced. Judging by his actions, owning knowledge concerning this mysterious entity might be a dangerous thing. Dangerous enough to end her life.

She had to prevent Robb from taking that final step. Making it home to Eric became her overriding goal.

"The Order? What are you talking about?" Emily swallowed hard while trying to stifle her emotions. "What's 'The Order?' What did you do to that trooper?"

"I had to protect myself." Robb opened the car door and dropped down behind the steering wheel again. "The Order of the Crimson Thorns wants me dead. This is the only way I can become strong enough to fight back."

"Strong enough? What do you mean?"

"Simple. I must absorb the life energies of seven people to become the Crimson Reaper. Only then will I have the power I need to bring down The Order."

"That's … How can you …"

"Only two are left. Then all this ugliness will end."

Emily stared at him in stunned silence. Visions of Robb lunging forward, subduing her, and stealing her life energy with his amulet flashed through her mind's eye. What could she do to stop him? Emily owned no ability to combat dark magic like her daughter-in-law did.

"I promise I won't drain your life energy from you," Robb said, cutting through the tense silence. "Every king needs a queen. All I want is for you to embrace your role at my side when the time arrives to make that choice."

He drew out the amulet from underneath his shirt and recited a brief incantation. Emily recognized some Latin words forming the spell, but their meaning eluded her. A purple glow passed from the strange cross into his hand. Robb released the amulet and leaned forward. He pressed his hand over her eyelids, forcing them shut.

Emily let out a sudden gasp and her eyelids popped open. She blinked rapidly and sat upright. Her head and neck had been kinked against the headrest like she woke from a deep slumber.

Did I fall asleep?

Emily didn't remember falling asleep. Come to think of it, she remembered nothing after they got into the sedan and drove away from the art center. She glanced out the window and massaged her stiff neck. A passing sign identified the road as the C-470 highway.

"Welcome back, sleepyhead."

Emily snapped her head toward Robb. He flashed an amiable grin at her before quickly shifting his gaze back to the road.

"I'm sorry," she said. "This is so embarrassing. Didn't realize I was that tired. I don't want to be a boring date."

His smile deepened.

"No worries. I don't mind boring dates."

18

Emily's body language told Eric a different story than her words. After his mom arrived home from her date with Cooper, she proclaimed how much fun she had checking out handmade pottery in Golden. Emily even proudly showed off two new acquisitions to add to her budding collection. Still, her smile straddled the boundary between natural and forced. Emily leaned against a chair at the kitchen table with slumped shoulders and fidgeted with her birthstone ring while they talked.

An anxious inner voice whispered to Eric, accusing his mom of hiding key details of her date from him. Something horrible happened as the evening progressed. He felt certain of this reality.

"Mom? Is everything okay?" Palpable concern infused his voice. "Did something happen to you?"

Emily straightened up, widened her smile, answered him with an abrupt dismissive wave.

"No. no. no. I'm fine," she said. "Robb and I had a fabulous time together. I got a little sleepy on the ride home. That's a bit embarrassing, but I guess I'm not the first person in the world to nap in a car before."

A crease formed in Eric's brow.

"Did he hurt you? You can tell me, Mom."

Her blue eyes hardened as though his implication of inappropriate or abusive behavior from her date deeply offended her.

"I'm fine," she repeated, more firmly this time. "If Robb was an abusive asshole, believe me, I'd let you and the rest of the world know."

Eric lacked confidence in her declaration well after retreating upstairs to his bedroom. His mom didn't have a spotless track record for being honest with herself or others about troubled relationships. What happened with his dad stood out as a prime example. Brant's infidelity blindsided Emily and shattered their once-happy family. She initially tried to hide the ugly facts from Eric and Ron. Emily only came clean and shared the full story several weeks after they restarted their lives in Deer Falls.

Details his mom shared about her date simply didn't add up in Eric's mind. No doubt that bastard did something awful to assure her silence. Eric found himself stuck walking an invisible tightrope without a safety net below. He needed to expose Cooper's crimes and make him face justice while not also endangering his mom's life or putting himself in jeopardy.

Max, Tatiana, and Devin all hung around until Emily arrived safely home. They all left soon afterward. Eric wished his friends had lingered at his house for a while longer. He needed a listening ear. A sounding board for all the anxious, troubled thoughts buzzing through his brain like persistent wasps. But he also needed more information. Knowledge that his friends, even with all their best efforts, could not provide.

Maybe searching out details about Cooper's strange cross through the right source would shed some much-needed light on the mystery surrounding him. Tatiana, Devin, and Max did their best to help him track down clues earlier in the evening. Even if they were skeptical about the reasons driving the search.

"So, Cooper sports some odd jewelry," Devin said. "What does it have to do with anything?"

Eric spun around in his desk chair and faced his friend. He shrugged.

"Don't know yet," he said. "But I think Cooper killed Trace. When Sheriff Leeds interrogated me about Trace's death, he asked me about that cross I saw around Cooper's neck."

"Cops wouldn't ask you about a detail like that if it didn't matter," Max replied.

Eric nodded and spun back around to his laptop.

There's a definite connection," he said, planting his fingertips on the touchpad. "We need to figure out what the connection is."

Eric opened a new search engine browser window and glanced over at his best friend again. Max rubbed his chin and cast his eyes at the ceiling.

"Do you suppose Cooper's cross is some sort of magical talisman?

Eric nodded and refocused his attention on the computer screen.

'That's my first guess," he said.

Tatiana instantly let out a sigh and pursed her lips.

"Why are you always so quick to come up with a supernatural explanation for everything that happens around here?"

Eric cast a side-eye glance at her and frowned.

"Because it usually turns out to be the right one."

Tatiana's skepticism became more warranted as their search dragged on. Few search engine results yielded useful information. They knew little about the origin of the cross or what purpose it served. The others gave up and called it a night when Eric's mom walked through the door seemingly unharmed. Eric refused to let himself rest. If Cooper was indeed a murderer as he suspected, doing nothing only promised to place his mom in tremendous danger.

Eric didn't find the answers he sought. But he knew at least one person who had a better idea of where to find these types of answers. Christina.

When he made a video call, Ron appeared on the other screen instead of her. Swell. Eric wasn't in the right frame of mind to talk to him.

"Hey, little bro." Ron glanced over at a wall off screen. "You're catching me kind of late over here. Can we chat in the morning?"

Eric pursed his lips and scowled at him.

Who was he trying to fool? Utah and Colorado were in the same damn time zone. Not only that, but Ron had been a night owl ever since he grew old enough to get away with being one.

"Yeah, I'm thrilled to see you too. Is Christina around? I need to talk to her."

"Like right now?"

"Yeah, it's an emergency."

Ron's lips curled into an inevitable smirk. He leaned back in his office chair.

"Is it the usual crazy shit in Deer Falls?"

"This is so much worse. In fact, I think what's going on might be Cassandra-level worse."

Eric's declaration erased his older brother's smile. Ron leaned forward in the chair and stared unblinking at his computer screen. Visible terror swam through his eyes as he ran his hand through his unruly brown hair.

"I'll tell my wife you need to chat with her."

He sprang out of the chair and hurried out of the room. Christina walked through the doorway a minute later. A concerned look spread over her face as she took a seat in front of her computer's camera.

"What's going on in Deer Falls?" she asked.

"My mom's new boyfriend is a murderer."

Christina's hazel eyes widened. She leaned forward in her chair.

"A murderer?" she repeated. "Who did he murder?"

"Trace Fowler died in a suspicious car accident a few days ago," Eric explained. "Then, the school canceled classes the rest of this week after they found Principal Reynolds dead in her office."

Christina let out a short gasp when he told her of both deaths and pressed a hand to her lips.

"So, how is your mom's new boyfriend connected to their deaths?"

"He's the assistant principal."

Christina shot Eric a puzzled look.

"Besides his job," she clarified. "Why would he kill both a student and the principal?"

"I don't really … know." Eric hesitated while he tried to reason out Cooper's motives in his mind. "I mean, Trace threatened to have his uncle sue him. But it seems like overkill to, you know, kill somebody over a lawsuit."

"Why did Trace threaten a lawsuit?"

"Cooper told me and him we'd both be suspended from the basketball team for a game after we got into a fight inside the gym."

Christina nodded and flashed a knowing frown.

"Welcome to my world," she said. "I spent as much time in detention as I did in some of my classes at that stupid school."

Eric recalled her stories about the steady verbal and emotional abuse she endured from other Deer Falls residents for being a witch. Some people used her magical nature as an excuse to pepper Christina with insults and snide jokes. Many others simply avoided interacting with her out of fear of what she would do if they angered her.

Whispered rumors about Christina still lingered in Deer Falls long after she and Ron left town to attend college at Denver University. It weighed heavy on Eric's soul after he got to know her and experienced Christina's kindness and thoughtfulness firsthand.

"Sheriff Leeds shared a key detail about Trace's death while questioning me a day later," Eric said. "He asked about a strange symbol he found and showed me a sketch of it. Then, I noticed Cooper sporting a necklace that matched the same symbol."

Christina raised her eyebrows.

"What's the symbol?"

"An odd-looking cross. I've never seen another cross like the one around Cooper's neck, to be honest. I'll show you what I mean."

Eric grabbed a notebook and a pen from his open backpack sitting next to the desk. He scribbled out a quick sketch of the cross from memory and snapped a photo with his smartphone.

'I'm sending a sketch of the symbol over to you," he said. "Maybe you'll have a better idea of what it means than I do."

"I'll give it my best shot," Christina replied.

Eric texted the photo to her. She glanced down at her phone a couple of seconds later and studied the sketch he sent. Christina's mouth dropped open.

Her eyes trailed back up to the video camera.

"I sure hope this isn't what I think it is."

Eric's throat tightened and he gulped. If this symbol inspired fear in an experienced witch like Christina, he knew it equaled bad news for him and his mom.

Horrible news.

She rose from her chair and pulled a thick hardcover book from a bookshelf against the adjacent wall. The tome's title — *The Essential Guide to Talismans and Totems* — was splashed in bold rounded letters across the front cover. Christina cracked open the book and scanned through several pages before stopping on a page one-third of the way through the volume.

"Oh no." Her voice grew quiet. "This isn't good at all."

Eric's heart pounded faster. Part of him didn't want to learn what she learned. If a safe place existed where the terrors of this world — or any other world — couldn't touch him, Eric would lock himself away in that spot for the rest of time.

No such place existed.

No other choice lay before him except to learn the strange symbol's true meaning.

"Where did that symbol come from?" Eric finally broke his silence with the question he feared to ask. "What does it mean?"

"According to this book, your assistant principal is in possession of the reaper amulet."

"What is the reaper amulet?"

Christina raised her eyes and fixed her gaze on the camera again. Worry swam through each one, drowning both iris and pupil.

"The reaper amulet is an ancient talisman housing unspeakable dark magic," she said. "Whoever unlocks its full power becomes The Crimson Reaper."

"The Crimson Reaper?" Eric repeated.

"One who wields the Crimson Reaper's powers can warp and reshape reality into whatever form suits their purposes," Christina said. "If your assistant principal unlocks the amulet's full powers, he can rule the entire world and bend it to his will."

Eric sank back against his chair as the full scope of her revelation enveloped his mind like a dark cloud. Rule the world? Through dark magic? Oh God. This situation was much worse than anything he first imagined.

Even worse than Cassandra returning.

"How do we stop him?"

Christina pressed her lips together and stared up at her ceiling. She seemed uncertain how to answer Eric.

"It won't be simple." Her eyes refocused on him again. "You need to find a way to steal that amulet."

Steal the amulet?

Her solution sounded like an impossible task. If this thing did what Christina said it did, no chance in hell Cooper would let it out of his sight. Even if he concocted a foolproof plan for snatching the amulet from Cooper's possession, Eric had no clue where he lived in Deer

Falls. Following him to his residence from the high school wouldn't work, since classes were not scheduled to resume until Monday at the earliest.

Tailing the assistant principal presented a huge risk from the start. What if Cooper spotted him? Eric hated to think what would happen if Cooper pieced together everything he was trying to do.

"You're asking me to do an impossible thing," Eric said. "If the amulet is so powerful, I'll bet he'll guard it with his life."

Christina fiddled with her ponytail and stole a glance at her bookshelf. She bit her lower lip, trying to hide a worried frown.

"I'll search for some protection spells that can counteract the amulet's magic," she said. "Do everything in your power to talk Emily out of seeing him again. Dating him is far too dangerous."

Eric snatched up his pen while she talked and chewed on the cap. Protecting his mom while stopping Cooper from executing his dark plan presented a huge dilemma. The whole situation weighed heavily on him.

What if he only made things worse?

"I can't do this alone," Eric said. "I need you here in Deer Falls."

"I wish I could be there. My hands are tied. Ron and I both have jobs — and we're also dealing with a troubling situation of our own unfolding out here."

"What do you mean? What's going on?"

Christina glanced down and away from the camera. She licked her lips nervously.

"You've already got enough on your plate," she said. "I shouldn't have mentioned it. Believe me when I say I can't be in two places at once."

Eric's eyes trailed over to her collection of books. A solution to their respective dilemmas suddenly popped into his head.

"Isn't there a magic spell where you can send yourself here without hopping on a plane to Colorado?"

Christina shot him a puzzled look again and slowly shook her head. A slight brief smile cracked through her worried demeanor.

"Do I look like a Jedi to you?"

Eric realized he made impossible demands on his sister-in-law, but his rising fears drove him to that end. Facing the prospect of combating his assistant principal on his own scared him to death. Magic didn't flow through Eric naturally like Christina. She was the sole reason he didn't lose his life to Cassandra six years ago.

Christina sensed those same fears.

"I won't leave you unprepared," she promised. "Give me a little time to do research and I'll send over a few spells to aid your cause."

"How soon?"

"As soon as I find the right ones. Until then, do everything possible to keep yourself and your mom safe."

Her promise of borrowed magic only partially soothed Eric's fraying nerves. Assuming this burden felt as daunting as challenging the Denver Nuggets to a pickup game with an intramural team. One specific thought gnawed on Eric. If he screwed up the spells Christina imparted to him, who would save his skin? None of his friends ever showcased any apparent magical abilities.

Not in front of him anyway.

"I'm not like you," Eric said. "You wield magic like a pro. I could never do even a fraction of what you do."

Christina leaned forward and met his concerns with a steady, reassuring smile.

"That's not true," she said. "You have a seed for magic already planted within you."

"How is that possible? I've never even cast a spell."

"A spark of divine essence lies within every human. Magic is a conduit to tap into this power."

"Divine power? Like a god?"

"We are all gods in embryo. Some are naturally gifted in magic. Others must learn magic through study and experience. But everyone can nourish that seed."

Christina's eyes brightened during her pep talk. Doubts lingered in his head, but Eric said nothing else beyond making a vow to do his best. He leaned back and cast his eyes up at the ceiling after their call ended and her video screen vanished. The prospect of trying to harness even a kernel of magic by himself sounded and felt terrifying. Still, what other choice did Eric have other than to embrace this new path ahead?

Only magic stopped magic.

Time to buckle up for a crash course in learning how to tap into his divine spark.

19

Watching and waiting outside the high school only fueled Eric's frustration. If he had an ability to snap his fingers and sweep Cooper out of his life, nothing would stop him from making it happen. Of course, if he wielded such power, asking for Christina's help in the first place would be unnecessary. Eric lacked any real power to stand against dark magic on his own. Intelligence and common sense were the only weapons he owned in this battle.

Patient thinking and planning equaled survival.

That still didn't mean Eric didn't want to skip to the end of this ordeal. If only stealing a magical amulet were as simple as knocking down a corner three late in a close basketball game or winding through a rugged tree-lined trail on his mountain bike. Cooper would never stand a chance.

Eric sat inside his car, seatbelt unbuckled, peering at the main doors with a pair of binoculars. He leaned forward and rested his elbows on the steering wheel.

A weary sigh escaped his lips.

"This feels like a colossal waste of time," Eric lowered the binoculars and glanced over at Tatiana in the passenger seat. "I'm really starting to think he's not here."

"My dad went to the school board meeting last night," she said. "He told me they cleared all teachers and administrators to return to the high school today."

"Are you sure that he wasn't just trying to distract you to avoid checkmate?"

Tatiana flashed a wide grin.

"He should stop sacrificing his queen if he wants to prevent that outcome."

Eric matched her smile with his own. He quickly learned not to challenge his friend to a game of chess. She always seemed to be at least five or six moves ahead of Eric before he advanced a single pawn. Tatiana credited her ability to logging lots of match time against older kids in her Ukrainian orphanage before she joined her new family in Deer Falls. None of the older orphans showed their opponents mercy whenever anyone put a chess board in front of them.

Neither did Tatiana.

"What do we do if he sees us out here spying on him?" Devin asked.

Eric frowned and raised his binoculars again. They were parked in the parking lot directly across the street from the high school. Even if Cooper had eagle eyes, no chance in hell he'd notice four teens sitting in a parked car watching him.

"I don't think we need to worry." Eric didn't bother to pry his eyes away to look at Devin. "I doubt Cooper will even glance in our direction on his way out of the school."

"Are you sure about that?" Max asked.

Eric lowered the binoculars and snapped his head at the backseat.

"If you think there's a better spot to spy on him, hit me with it."

Max shrugged and said nothing.

"That's what I thought," Eric said, refocusing his attention on the main doors.

His friends were simply growing nervous — matching the tension tying his own body in knots. They hung out inside this car for close to an hour now without any sign of Cooper. Still, he had to be here inside the high school based on the intel Tatiana gathered from her father. Cars dotted a handful of spaces throughout the faculty parking lot. Odds were favorable at least one vehicle belonged to Cooper himself.

"What we need to do is go get more donuts," Max said, dissipating the growing silence. "You can't have a good stakeout without a steady supply of snacks."

Eric stole a glance over his shoulder. An empty rectangular box lay wedged between Max and Devin on the backseat. Bits of frosting and sprinkles dotting cardboard were lone remnants from their first coffee shop donut run.

"We better hang tight," he said. "You know he'll come through those doors the second I start the car and peel out of here. And then we'll have missed our chance."

Tatiana mirrored Eric and raised her own pair of binoculars. Silence blanketed the car again. Eric started drumming his fingers against the top of the steering wheel. This stakeout had taken much longer than he hoped or anticipated. Would enough daylight be left to follow him effectively once Cooper finally emerged from the school?

"We need some tunes." Devin finally cut through the silence. "I got a killer playlist I can pull up."

Eric smiled.

"Yeah. If it slaps —"

He paused mid-sentence. One of the main entrance doors pushed outward. Cooper popped through the open doorway a moment later, toting a briefcase.

"And there he is," Tatiana said.

Eric trailed the assistant principal to the faculty parking lot with his binoculars, never shifting his gaze away from him for even a second. Cooper shifted his briefcase from his right hand to his left and fished a fob out of his front pants pocket. Headlights flashed. Eric made silent notes on the vehicle's appearance. A run-of-the-mill brown sedan.

Dented bumper. Patches of rust on the back fenders.

Cooper climbed into the sedan. Lights illuminated a second time when he started the engine. The sedan backed up, executed a K-turn, and sped toward the street in front of the school.

"That's our cue to exit," Max said.

Eric nodded and turned the key in the ignition. The engine coughed and shook for a few seconds before settling into a normal hum. He waited until Cooper's sedan turned west onto Nickel Canyon Road before pulling out of the senior parking lot and taking off in the same direction. Eric blew through the stop sign while making the same turn. An agitated horn from another westbound vehicle greeted the four teens.

"Whoa!" Tatiana dropped her binoculars and gasped. She gripped the sides of her seat. "Dude, this isn't a high-speed chase!"

"We gotta keep up," Eric said.

"I don't want to crash and die while tailing him," she replied.

Eric scowled and said nothing. But he reduced his speed as soon as they were within a couple of car lengths of the sedan. The winter sun hung low on the horizon, but enough light remained to not complicate visibility. They tailed Cooper as his sedan cut a path through the heart of Deer Falls.

Nickel Canyon Road to Main Street.

Main Street to Topaz Lane.

"I think he's heading over to Leaftown Manor," Tatiana said.

Her suspicions were confirmed when the brown sedan pulled into a parking spot in front of a Victorian-style house on Topaz Lane. The house functioned as a quaint bed-and-breakfast inn. Eric found it strange that Cooper had not rented an actual apartment or house by now. Almost as though he intended to flee from Deer Falls at a moment's notice. Eric traveled further up the narrow street and found a parking spot a half-block away on the opposite side of the street. He wanted to avoid drawing undue attention while staying close enough to still see Cooper's activities.

The assistant principal sprang from his car, with briefcase in hand, and darted up a stone path to the inn's front door. Cooper glanced over both shoulders, first up the street and then down Topaz Lane. He never made eye contact with Eric's car. Still, the fact Cooper even looked in their direction only tightened Eric's nerves.

Those spells Christina sent him better work how they were supposed to work.

Eric printed off a PDF attachment from her email containing several pages' worth of instructions. Christina uncovered numerous helpful incantations. Some were designed to protect his mind and body from harm. Others were meant to aid Eric in obtaining the amulet and neutralizing its dark magic.

"Hand me the bag with all the spells, crystals, and candles." He turned and faced Tatiana. "This is as good of a time as any to track the amulet."

Tatiana snatched up a purple gift bag from between her knees and handed it over to Eric.

"I still think all this hocus pocus stuff is a total waste of time," she said. "We should go to the police and tell them the information your sister-in-law gave you."

Eric met her suggestion with a dismissive hand wave. He was not in the right mood to deal with her never-ending skepticism.

"How will they stop him?" he asked. "And supposing for a second they do succeed, are we better off with the sheriff having this amulet?"

"Not a chance," Max said.

Eric gave him an appreciative nod.

"Thank you, bro. Glad somebody else in here speaks my language."

He combed through the bag and drew out a thin broad crystal, a stout medium white candle, and a stapled document chronicling all of Christina's collected spells. Eric handed the crystal and candle to

Tatiana. She scrunched up her face and released it into a puzzled look.

"Why are you giving these to me?" she asked.

"Just hold them for a second while I find the spell we're supposed to use." His tone grew cross. "You don't need to do anything else."

Eric flipped through multiple pages, poring over each spell. Figuring out what each one was supposed to do proved easier said than done. He went through all the pages twice before finally settling on one listed on the fourth page of the document.

"This is supposed to be some sort of tracking spell." Eric raised his chin and cast his eyes at Max and Devin. "Let's see if it works."

"Tracking spell?" Devin repeated. "What's it supposed to track? Cooper? His jewelry?"

"Says here it detects and tracks mystical objects," Eric said. "I guess the amulet qualifies as one."

He slid his eyes back over to Tatiana. She didn't bother to conceal an annoyed frown.

"Hand me the crystal again."

Tatiana passed it back to him. Eric grasped the crystal tight inside his palm.

"All I need to do is specify what we're seeking and recite the spell into this crystal," he said. "Then the crystal's supposed to take care of the rest."

Eric studied the tracking spell, reading each word three times to commit it to memory. He drew a deep breath and stared intently at the crystal.

Find the reaper amulet.

Reveal to us the way.

Track the deep essence.

Show us where it lay.

A simple incantation. Why did it not feel simple when he spoke? Each word rolled off Eric's tongue in a labored cadence. His fingers trembled around the crystal. A dull glow peeked out from between each one.

"Ow!"

The crystal dropped from Eric's hand suddenly and bounced off his binoculars. It landed in an empty cup holder. He pressed his fingertips to his lips. A sudden jolt of energy zapped his whole hand like static electricity.

"I think it's working," Max said. "Look at the crystal!"

He pointed to the crystal's landing spot. A distinct blue-green light emanated from it now. The light climbed from the crystal and spread out with the consistency of a thick mist over the seat between Eric and Tatiana. Soon, a distinct jagged crimson dot coalesced within the crystal's aura. Details filled in around the dot revealing outlines of assorted furniture within a bedroom. A peculiar sensation gripped Eric as though he watched an invisible hand sketch with an invisible pencil within the light.

"This can't be real."

He glanced at Tatiana. Her mouth dropped open and her eyes widened as she stared at the scene unfolding within the light. Eric let loose a brief smile when he saw her reaction.

This is how skepticism dies.

His eyes were drawn back to the mysterious room. Every detail inside the room grew sharper and gained greater definition until it resembled a translucent negative like an old photograph. The crimson dot soon settled on a broad pillow propped against a headboard and did not budge from that spot.

"That's it." Eric jabbed a finger at the jagged dot. Light emanating from the crystal flickered around his top knuckle. "That has to be the amulet."

"Wicked," Devin said. "Do you have a spell that'll zap it from his room to your car?"

His question raised Eric's hopes. This little heist would go much smoother if they took possession of the amulet without entering the inn. Did Christina include such a spell among the ones she sent over to him? Eric thumbed through the spells. He found protection spells and binding spells and an incantation to lock the amulet once they had possession.

None were designed to transport the amulet itself.

"I can't find one," Eric said. "We'll have to figure out a different way to steal it from Cooper."

Only one possibility for obtaining the amulet lay before them. Eric danced around saying it aloud because going down that path entailed considerable danger. His friends all had a similar thought cross their minds, judging by their faces. Nervous frowns sprouted as they collectively gazed at the jagged crimson dot.

"Someone has to go inside that room." Max put into words a terrifying realization gripping all four teens. "If we can't transport the amulet out here, then we don't really have a better option."

"I'll go."

Eric didn't hesitate to volunteer. Cooper had to be stopped one way or another before he executed his plan. The last thing Deer Falls needed was another all-powerful murderer terrorizing the town.

Especially one who was dating his mom.

"We seriously need to call the police." Tatiana drew her phone out of her purse. "I'm serious. This is dangerous. Let them handle this mess."

"No." Eric shook his head and reached out to push her phone down. "They will be powerless against him."

"What about you?" Tatiana shifted the phone away from his grasp. "I don't want you to get hurt."

"I have to protect my mom," Eric said.

At once, the rear passenger side door popped open. Max slid off the backseat and planted both feet on the asphalt.

"Wait! Where are you going?" Eric stretched out his arm. "Get back in the car."

Max turned and ducked his head down.

"You've got a protection spell among those spells Christina sent you, right?" he asked. "Just use one on me and I'll be in and out of there."

He snapped his fingers to emphasize his confidence in the spell. Eric's throat tightened and he licked his lips. Where did this sudden bravado come from?

"I can't ask you to do this, Max. You —"

"I don't want anything bad to happen to your mom either," his friend said, interrupting him. "Let's do a video call once I go inside, so I have extra eyes and ears with me the whole time."

Max pushed the car door shut behind him and raced up the stone path. An anxious silence seeped into the car while everyone watched him open the front door and walk inside. Eric flipped through the collected spells before stopping on a protection spell.

"Hand me the candle," he said, looking up at Tatiana.

She returned the white candle to Eric. He swallowed hard and his nerves tightened like guitar strings. Max's safety depended on him getting this right. Eric drew a deep breath and recited the words, inserting Max's name at the right spot.

Spirits, light this candle.

Let its burning flame

shield Max from dark forces,

both seen and unseen,

and light his path ahead.

When Eric said the final word, a splinter of light shot out from the crystal at the candle. A flame spontaneously ignited on the wick. Tatiana and Devin both gasped. Eric perched the candle atop the center of the dashboard.

His smartphone buzzed. Eric dug it out of his pocket and saw Max's number on the screen. He immediately swiped the screen, answered, and switched over to video call mode.

"Just enacted the protection spell," Eric said. "Do you feel any different?"

Max turned the video camera toward himself and cracked a forced nervous grin.

"Nah, am I supposed to feel different?"

He flipped his own smartphone around to allow Eric to see the inn's lobby through the video feed. Eric held the phone out toward the candle, so everything was also visible to Tatiana and Devin. Nobody stood or sat behind the check-in desk. The lobby's emptiness only piled on the dread already crawling under Eric's skin and over his bones like a legion of bugs scurrying out from under an overturned rock.

"Check the computer at the desk and see which room he's staying in," Tatiana said.

Max hurried behind the desk and followed her instructions. When he found the room number, he snatched a spare key card from a cubby hole on the wall behind the desk and climbed a set of carpeted stairs.

"Heading to room 2D, guys." Max lowered his voice to a whisper to avoid drawing extra attention to himself. "Keep your eyes peeled."

Eric's eyes jumped back and forth between the candle and his phone screen. As long as a flame stayed on the wick, Max stayed safe. His heart pounded faster when his friend stopped in front of a door at the end of the second-floor hallway.

"Do you see anyone near the amulet?" Max whispered. "I don't want to walk into an ambush."

Eric snapped his head toward the crimson dot. It stayed stationary in the same place as before. No sign of movement or an outline of a human figure near the bed or anywhere else in the room.

"The coast is clear," he said. "You're good to go, bro."

Max inserted the spare key card in the proper slot and gingerly turned the knob. He pushed back the door with his fingertips and crept through the open doorway. The phone's camera captured a panoramic view of a cramped bedroom decorated with vintage furniture. Sounds of water blasting from a shower seeped out from behind a closed bathroom door.

"I think he's taking a shower," Max said. "We caught a lucky break."

Eric exhaled sharply. They could use a little luck. Still, this spell had a limited shelf life. They needed to act fast.

"Do you see the amulet?" he asked.

Max focused his phone's video feed squarely on the bed. The same strange cross Eric saw Cooper sporting at his house lay unmoved from the pillow.

"Right where it's supposed to be." Max instantly grabbed the amulet and stuffed it inside a front coat pocket. "On my way out."

Zero resistance.

Eric exchanged nervous glances with Tatiana and Devin. An ominous feeling gripped him down to his bones. This amulet heist had worked out exactly like they had drawn it up. Everything went according to plan a little too perfectly.

All light emanating from the crystal suddenly vanished from Eric's peripheral vision. His eyes slid up to the candle. Smoke rose from the space a flame once occupied. The candle had been extinguished.

"Oh, God! The protection spell broke down," Eric said in a frantic whisper. "Get out of there now!"

Max's phone camera bounced from the vibrations as he sprinted toward the stairs. His breaths grew heavier and panicked. When Max reached the top of the stairs, he unleashed a frightened shout and lurched forward with violence. Carpet, the railing, and flailing limbs crossed through a jumbled video feed. When the feed stabilized again, the camera pointed at the ceiling. Pained groans mixed with cries escaped from Max.

"You took something that doesn't belong to you." A shadow darkened the camera for a second. "Didn't your parents ever teach you it's wrong to steal?"

Cooper.

Eric instantly recognized the assistant principal's voice on the other end. He grabbed the spell master document and frantically flipped back to the page containing the protection spell again.

"You need to be punished," Cooper said. "I'm afraid detention isn't the solution."

A sickening snap greeted Eric's ears. Purplish light flickered across the screen less than a minute later.

Max's labored breaths fell silent.

Tatiana unleashed a terrified scream and instantly dialed 911 on her phone. The assistant principal plucked Max's phone off the floor and stared into the camera. He glanced downward briefly and cracked a menacing grin.

"I hope you learned your lesson," Cooper said. "When I finally claim the amulet's full powers, I will find you and deal with you next."

The video feed stopped a second later.

Sobs choked Tatiana's voice and she stumbled over multiple words as she tried to talk to the 911 dispatcher. Devin buried his face deep in his hands and echoed her cries. Tears rolled down Eric's cheeks and splashed on the words forming the protection spell. His lips trembled as he turned the key in the ignition.

He failed.

He failed to protect his best friend when it counted. That failure cost Max his life.

20

Eric's car peeled away from the inn at highway speed. He blasted through a red light and turned down Main Street, ignoring angry horns and screeching brakes from oncoming vehicles. Did Cooper know from the start they were following him? Circumstances for nabbing the amulet were set up too perfectly in hindsight. If he indeed laid a trap, they stupidly took the bait with fatal consequences. Eric kept his foot pressed on the gas pedal and raced down the street to the sheriff's office.

They needed help. Then they needed to find a safe place to hide — if such a place even existed.

Their lives depended on it.

Going back to their classes on Monday morning was no longer an option. Cooper would only set another trap if they set foot inside the school and murder them one by one like he did to Max and Trace. Who knows how many people in Deer Falls and beyond had already died at his hand? All innocent victims to his dark rage.

"God, he's going to try to murder all of us, isn't he?"

The same degree of terror infused into Devin's voice laced through Eric from head to toe. Guilt settled on him in equal measure. This was all his fault. Blame fell on his shoulders alone. He dragged his friends into this fight, thoroughly unprepared to match wits with a cold-blooded killer skilled in dark magic.

Eric mashed down on the brake as he approached the sheriff's office. He swung the car into an open parking space across the street. Both passenger side tires rubbed against the curb as the vehicle came to a sudden jerky stop parallel to the sidewalk.

"We're outside the sheriff's office." Tatiana cast a frantic glance over her shoulder as she spoke with the 911 dispatcher. "I don't know if he followed us here or not. Please hurry."

She nodded vigorously a couple of times and burst into tears anew after the call ended.

"They said … to stay … inside the car." Tatiana trembled as she forced the words out. "The sheriff is … coming out here."

Eric faced his friend and grasped her hand tight. She pinched her eyelids shut and tried to slow her breathing. Mascara formed streaks down her cheeks, flushed from her eyelashes down a tear-carved path. He gnawed on his lower lip and tried to prevent fresh tears from bubbling to the surface.

I can't let Max die for nothing.

Despair took Eric hostage after that thought barged into his head. What could he do to avenge Max's death? Every spell Christina sent him was practically useless without a natural ability to harness magic like her.

Rap. Rap. Rap.

The three startled teens nearly jumped out of their seats. Eric let go of Tatiana's hand and turned toward the driver's side window. Sheriff Leeds stood on the other side. He cocked his head at him and wore a concerned frown. Eric pressed a button and lowered his window.

"He murdered … Max."

Eric choked up while saying his best friend's name and wrapped his fingers tight around the steering wheel.

"I'm so sorry, son." Leeds carried a sympathetic lilt in his voice. More of a fatherly tone than a sheriff's tone. "Can you tell me exactly what happened?"

Eric drew in a deep calming breath as he worked to gather his thoughts. He didn't want to omit a single detail concerning the events that unfolded which might help bring that evil bastard to justice.

"Cooper did it," Devin blurted out. "You need to hurry and go arrest him."

Leeds stepped back from the open window. A nervous fear flashed through his eyes and his frown deepened.

"Robb Cooper? Your assistant principal?"

Eric answered his question with a vigorous nod.

"He ambushed Max inside Leaftown Manor," he said. "Everything happened so fast."

"Our dispatcher just sent over two deputies," Leeds said. "Is Robb Cooper still inside the inn?"

Eric swallowed hard and shifted in his seat. Were they already too late? Cooper must have fled the scene, right? The last thing he'd ever do is stick around and allow cops to haul him away in handcuffs before he unlocked that amulet's full power.

"We didn't see him walk outside before we left," Tatiana said, finally breaking her silence.

"Did he also attack any of you?

"No," she said. "I don't think he saw us."

"What happened? What were you and the Thompson boy all doing at Leaftown Manor?"

Eric ran his hands through his hair and pinched his eyelids shut for a moment while pondering the sheriff's questions. Should he reveal what he learned about the reaper amulet? Leeds and other Deer Falls cops were far from trustworthy given their track record with past supernatural events. They feigned ignorance of magic while doing everything possible to conceal its existence. Still, Eric welcomed whatever help available to him. Not telling the sheriff what he suspected concerning Cooper's plans posed much less danger than keeping quiet.

"This isn't his first murder," Eric said, ignoring the sheriff's question. "I think he killed Trace too. It's all connected to that strange symbol you showed me."

The sheriff furrowed his brow.

"What did you say?"

"The reaper amulet," Eric clarified. "Cooper was wearing it yesterday when he dropped by my house to pick my mom up for a date."

Leeds froze.

"We found out it's some sort of magic weapon," Devin said. "He can use the amulet to take over the world."

"We tried to steal it away from him," Tatiana added. "Max swiped it from his room. Cooper found out and killed him before he made it back outside."

Her voice broke again as she recounted Max's fate. The sheriff quickly radioed one of his deputies and asked if they had encountered Cooper inside Leaftown Manor. A deputy answering Leeds revealed they found a deceased teenage male crumpled against a bottom stair in the lobby. A subsequent room-to-room search turned up no signs of the assistant principal anywhere on the premises. Overhearing their conversation only increased Eric's terror and furthered the despair taking root inside of him.

Cooper evaded the cops and escaped the inn.

"We'll find Robb Cooper and arrest him." Leeds refocused his attention on the three teens. "He'll face justice for what he did today. You have my word."

"What about our families?" Tatiana asked. "What if he comes after my mom and dad and my sister?"

"We'll post deputies outside each of your homes," Leeds said. "The best thing you can do now is go home and shelter in place until Cooper is in our custody."

Tatiana cast a frantic glance over her shoulder in the direction of Topaz Lane.

"But what if he follows —"

"I will personally escort you back to your homes," Leeds said, interrupting her. "We won't let him hurt you."

The sheriff's vow did nothing to ease Eric's concerns for his safety or his friends' safety. Cooper broke through a protection spell to steal Max's life. He already showed an ability to counteract magic with ease, so taking down any cops blocking his path would be a simple thing.

Once Leeds returned to his patrol car, Eric started the engine again and headed for his house. Driving through downtown Deer Falls with the sheriff following a car length behind offered zero comfort. Eric wished for Tatiana to be right. God, he wanted to convince himself Cooper saw only Max and everyone else escaped that murdering bastard's notice.

His instincts told him a different story.

Eric made it home within a few minutes, but each minute took forever until he pulled his car into the driveway. Flooring the gas pedal crossed his mind more than once. Eric resisted the temptation. The sheriff taking on an impromptu bodyguard role likely didn't include a temporary exemption from speeding tickets. Driving under the speed limit felt agonizing. It functioned almost like an open invitation for Cooper to come catch him.

The garage door was closed when Eric pulled into the driveway and parked. No visible signs of other vehicles in the immediate vicinity, aside from his friends' cars parked along the street. Renewed grief attacked Eric when his eyes fell on Max's stationary vehicle. What would he tell his parents? They would never forgive him for what happened to their son. Such an outcome seemed inevitable and appropriate.

Eric didn't feel like he deserved forgiveness.

He drew the key out of the ignition and blinked back fresh tears. Tatiana extended her hand this time and slipped it inside his hand. Sadness etched itself into every part of her face.

"I have no right to ask this of you, but I need your help." Eric's eyes shifted from Tatiana to Devin and then back to her as he spoke. "I need you both to come inside with me and check on my mom before you leave. If anything happened to her —"

"We won't abandon you," Devin said, interrupting him. "That's not what friends do."

Tatiana agreed with a silent nod. Eric returned a brief appreciative half-smile. All three teens slid out of the car and planted feet on cement right as Leeds pulled up in his cruiser. His door popped open.

"Where are you all going?" Leeds called out as he climbed out of the patrol car. "We need to get you home to your families quickly."

Eric stopped at the edge of the snow-encrusted front lawn and turned to face him.

"Cooper started dating my mom a while back," he said. "We all want to make sure she's safe before they head out of here."

Leeds glanced past his shoulder at the front door and let out a worried sigh.

"Wait for me." He pushed his car door shut. "We'll check on her together."

Leeds caught up to Eric, Tatiana, and Devin and trudged with them across the lawn and up the front porch steps. Four distinct icy wisps formed as the tension turned their breaths heavier in the frozen air. Shadows devoured every inch of space now that the sun had dipped below the horizon. Lingering twilight began undertaking a similar retreat from the sky. A porch light and flood lights over the garage kept darkness from completely shrouding the house. The sheriff drew back the screen door and raised a closed fist, intending to wrap his knuckles against the front door.

Eric waved him off.

"We've got a doorbell and, better yet, I have my own key," he said.

Leeds stepped back and beckoned him forward with a sweeping hand. Eric unlocked both deadbolt and doorknob and pushed the door open. Silence greeted him when he stepped into the house. No lights were turned on inside the living room or Emily's office. Light only peeked out from the kitchen.

"Mom! Are you home?"

Eric flipped on the light switch. Light from a swinging overhead lamp diffused through the front room. His question received no answer. Leeds pressed the thumb release on his holster and drew his pistol.

"Mrs. Olson, this is Sheriff Leeds," he said. "I'm here with your son. If you can hear us, please come out here where we can see you."

Leeds approached the kitchen and motioned for Eric, Tatiana, and Devin to stay back. He ducked inside the doorway and his head turned one way and then the other.

"Clear." He glanced over his shoulder. "You're safe to come in here."

A glimmer of hope rising within Eric quickly got snuffed out again when he entered the room. No sign of his mom anywhere downstairs. Where did she go? Visions of Cooper abducting his mom began to crowd out other thoughts formerly occupying Eric's head.

A note taped to the refrigerator door caught his eye. His heart raced faster. A chill dug deep into every bone.

Oh God. Not this.

Please not this.

Eric's worst fears were coming true, one after another. He yanked the note out from under a Pizza Wagon magnet and unfolded the lined yellow paper.

Going to a movie with Robb at Center Street Cinema. I left some money on the counter. Order yourself a pizza for dinner.

Eric lowered the note and spotted a $20 bill sitting on the kitchen island. Tremors seized both of his hands. Emily willingly put herself in a murderer's clutches. A killer who used the pretense of going on another date to lure her away from the house and safety. The chances of Emily enjoying a fun, normal date — or returning home alive — were zero.

Eric refused to let himself lose his best friend and his mom to the same killer on the same day. No time left to do anything except act.

His mom's life hinged on Eric reaching her before Cooper turned her into his next victim.

21

All eyes inside the kitchen fixed on Eric when he let his mom's note drop to his side. Their faces mirrored an unrestrained panic growing inside him — a terror which refused to be satiated. Even without speaking, a universal awareness filled the room. Their ordeal had only entered the beginning stages.

The worst part? Emily placed herself at the epicenter of the unfolding nightmare.

"My mom is with Cooper." Eric dipped his head and spoke in a hushed tone. "She said they went out to the movies."

Tatiana gasped.

"He can't be that dumb," Devin said.

She snapped her head over at him. Eric simply nodded. Cooper going on a casual date with his mom after what he did to Max seemed a little far-fetched. Surely, he wouldn't be that reckless and arrogant.

"Why would he kill Max and go to the movies like nothing happened?" Devin continued. "I don't buy it. I'll bet he abducted her and they're on the run. My guess is they're on their way out of —"

"I know," Eric said, meeting his gaze as he interrupted Devin. "We need to get out of here and go save her. Like right now."

Leeds cleared his throat and pointed at his own chest.

"I need to save her." His finger turned and pointed at Eric next. "You need to stay here."

"Wait." Tatiana raised her hand. "What about —"

"You two need to go home before your parents get worried about you." Leeds cut her off while first pointing to Tatiana and then Devin. "I wouldn't be doing my job if I turned a blind eye while three panicking teens run off to chase down a suspected serial killer. We don't need more families burying dead children around these parts."

No one voiced opposition to what the sheriff said but Eric raged at him silently. Sitting inside this empty house and waiting for someone else to rescue his mom bordered on pure torture. It also wasn't a choice he would be compelled to make.

Eric helped save his mom's life after Cassandra abducted her all those years ago because he refused to stay home. That awful witch overpowered his mom's original rescue party and cocooned everyone in life-sapping vines until he showed up with Max to cut them loose. Eric couldn't live with himself if he abandoned his mom to face a dark fate this time around. He drew out his smartphone and fired off a quick text to Tatiana and Devin once Leeds started for the front door.

Circle back after he leaves.

I'll leave the back door unlocked.

Buzzing sounds emanated from their pockets. Both Tatiana and Devin pulled out their phones and swiped the screens. They both glanced back up at Eric and silently acknowledged his unspoken plan.

"Let's go." Leeds turned back when he reached the door and beckoned them forward. "And if I see you three anywhere else in town tonight, there will be hell to pay."

Eric exchanged silent knowing glances with both friends. They put away their phones and obeyed the sheriff's instructions to follow him out the door. When the door shut behind them again, Eric sprang into action. He pulled up the maps app on his phone and studied likely routes Cooper might use to flee Deer Falls. They had to move quickly. Cooper got a big enough head start for Eric to worry about being able to head him off and rescue his mom.

Fleeing from Colorado to Utah popped into Eric's mind once he found a way to extract her from Cooper's grasp. Maybe he should contact Christina again and ask her to create a more potent protection spell. One powerful enough to buy enough time to escape from Deer Falls. Then Eric and his mom could join Christina and Ron in Utah and make a stand together if Cooper pursued them across state lines.

Eric still had the list of spells from Christina sitting in his car. Various items stored around the house — once paired with the right spells — would hopefully impede Cooper if he pursued them back here. Christina stockpiled a bunch of supplies, shortly before she and Ron got married, to prepare for future emergencies. Nothing defined an emergency for Eric more than his current situation.

He checked his text messages.

No word from either Tatiana or Devin yet.

Eric left the kitchen and walked past the hall closet to check the back door. He unlocked the knob and peeked his head outside. His eyes trailed across the backyard. No fresh footprints making a path across the hardened snow.

A car engine shut off near the street. Eric cocked his head toward the backyard fence. Did his friends make it back here already?

"Tatiana?" he called out. "Devin?"

No answer. No silence either. A car door slammed shut. Footsteps approached the backyard. Distinctive crunching across the snow. Eric braced himself against the half-open door and folded his arms.

"Hey guys, is that you?"

A short cough followed his question. Eric wasn't the one who coughed. His muscles tightened and his heartbeat quickened as a horrifying thought clawed into his head.

What if it wasn't his friends he heard?

"Say something." Eric licked his lips and raised his voice. "Don't keep me in suspense."

Devin finally appeared from around the corner and cracked a brief smile. Eric let out a relieved sigh.

"Sorry. Just making sure the sheriff hadn't doubled back after I did."

"Is Tatiana behind you?"

Devin wheeled around and stared back at the driveway.

"Hey, Tatiana are you behind me?"

"My sides are splitting." She answered him in a cross, slightly breathless voice. "Don't quit your day job."

Tatiana entered Eric's line of sight a few seconds later. Both teens trudged across the backyard snow and followed Eric back inside his house. He locked the door behind them.

"What's your plan?" Tatiana asked.

"I'm going to print off more copies of Christina's spells and a list of things we need to create protective barriers," Eric said. "While you and Devin are setting those up, I'll go find my mom and bring her home."

"How are you going to get him away from her by yourself?" Devin cast a worried glance at the back door as he posed the question. "If we're here and you're there —"

"I'll find a way," Eric said, cutting him off. He pressed a hand down on Devin's shoulder. "We need to prepare for what lies ahead. That's the only way we all have a chance to survive the night."

After Eric printed the necessary documents upstairs, he raced out of the house and drove toward the main highway leading out of town. His route took him down Center Street toward Main Street. When he passed by the movie theater, Eric instinctively glanced over at a tiny adjacent parking lot.

Cooper's vehicle was parked in the lot.

Same make and model. Same color. Same license plate.

Every detail matched.

How arrogant and foolish was this dude? Did he not fear the cops?

Eric supposed he didn't fear any potential adversary now. He had already gotten away with multiple murders. Cooper probably believed he'd stand against anyone with the aid of his dark magic.

The theater marquee displayed 6 pm and 9 pm showtimes for a new romantic comedy. Eric parked his car and glanced down at his phone. The 6 pm showing started only a few minutes ago.

I need to draw Mom out of the theater while the movie is playing. That's my window.

Reuniting with his mom and spiriting her away was only a first step. Hopefully, a few minutes passed before Cooper figured out Emily left the theater. Once he did, what was the next step? That murderous bastard would surely race to Eric's house and try to finish what he had started with Max earlier.

Survive the night.

His earlier words to Devin popped back into his head. Trying to survive the night was a scenario Eric hoped and prayed he and his mom would never have to face again.

Those prayers had gone unanswered.

* * *

Emily grimaced when her shoe pressed against a sticky substance coating the floor. Remnants of spilled soda. Some careless and lazy soul chose to let the soda dry where it first puddled rather than mop up the wasted drink. She counted herself fortunate that a discarded wad of gum wasn't the substance under foot. Digging that junk off the bottom of a shoe was tedious.

"These are great seats."

Robb flashed a satisfied grin as he glanced back at her. He cradled a medium tub of popcorn inside his elbow and held a medium root beer in the other hand. Emily carried a medium cola and a box of Reese's

Pieces — her favorite movie theater snacks.

"Back row always has the best seats in the house," she said. "I never sit close to the screen. Who wants to crane their neck for two hours to watch a movie?"

His smile deepened and he settled into his seat.

"We don't want anything to interfere with us enjoying this movie."

Emily returned his smile and handed him her candy while she stuck her soda in the cup holder on the arm of her chair. She unzipped her coat, laid it across the empty chair on her opposite side and dropped her purse on top. Robb passed the candy-filled box back to Emily as soon as she took her seat.

"Thank you."

She leaned forward and her lips met his. Their lips lingered in a warm and wet embrace until Emily pulled back again.

"We better save a little for the movie." She said, batting her eyelashes at him.

Robb nodded and sank back against his seat. Her eyes darted over to the screen. Emily felt a bit sheepish as she gazed forward. In her mid-40s with two older kids and she started acting like a horny teenager the minute she stepped inside a mostly empty movie theater. Eric would probably pantomime gagging and retching if he ever found out she kissed his assistant principal in public.

A movie trailer played on the screen. Deafening explosions. Car chases. All scenes drawn from an upcoming spy flick. Emily leaned forward in her chair a bit and smiled when the lead actor popped up in the trailer. She loved the first two movies in this series. The third one also looked promising at first glance.

As she watched a sniper assassinate a target behind their car, her eyes widened. A panicked chill raced down her spine. Random images flashed through her mind. Blinding headlights. A trembling cop splayed on the highway pavement. An unnatural eerie purple light spreading throughout Robb's face.

Emily let out a sudden terrified gasp.

"What's wrong?" Robb's hand instantly touched her forearm. "Are you feeling okay?"

His touch only increased her inner chill. Did she see him murder a cop earlier? Oh God. What did he intend to do to her?

She turned her head and met Robb's gaze.

Her mind went blank.

Emily blinked rapidly and shook her head. Where was she? Robb stared at her with concern flooding his eyes. She studied her surroundings. They were inside a darkened movie theater. That's right. She and Robb were out on a date. Checking out a new romantic comedy on opening weekend.

"It's nothing." Her eyes slid back to his. "Just some weird butterflies in my stomach."

Robb smiled and slid her hand into his hand.

"Do you need water?" He pointed at a curtain-covered exit with his head. "I'll go back out to concessions and buy you a bottle before the movie starts."

She flashed a polite smile and shook her head again.

"No thank you. I think I'll be fine. Maybe I just need to sip on my cola for a little while."

Robb nodded and leaned back in his chair.

"The offer stands if you change your mind."

Emily let herself relax again and settled deeper into her seat as studio and production company logos flashed across the big screen. A powerful urge to make out with Robb welled up inside her only a few minutes into the movie. She scooted closer to him. Robb set his popcorn aside and wrapped his arm around Emily's shoulder. She gazed up at him through her eyelashes. He dipped his chin and tilted his head. Their lips parted while making contact. Robb drew her bottom lip inside his mouth and held for a second before releasing again. Emily slipped her tongue inside his mouth, pressing the tip against his tongue. It felt so good. She wanted to freeze time and linger all night within this moment.

A strain of music cut through the back row. It didn't originate from the theater speakers. Angry whispers and shushes greeted the music. Emily pulled away from Robb and glanced over at her purse. She groaned. A romantic moment spoiled because she forgot to silence her cell phone before the movie started.

"I'm sorry," Emily whispered. "I better see who's calling. Might be an emergency."

She leaned over and grabbed her purse. Vibrations pulsated through her hand when she reached inside and wrapped her fingers around the phone. Emily glanced down at the screen when she drew it out. A missed call notification and a text message alert. An unfamiliar number accompanied the missed call notification.

The text came from her son.

Emily swiped the screen and clicked on Eric's text. Her eyes grew as wide as plates as she read his message.

Your boyfriend murdered Max.

Go out to the lobby.

HURRY!!!

She quickly stuffed the phone back inside the purse. Emily bit down on her lower lip to prevent a tremor from slipping out. She snapped her eyelids shut and dared not make eye contact with Robb. Oh God. Did he really murder Max? Eric and Max were best friends from day one in Deer Falls. Why would anyone do something so awful and evil to an innocent teenager? Robb seemed like such a sweet guy. Committing such a horrific crime didn't track with his personality.

Eric seemed uncomfortable with the whole notion of her dating Robb from the beginning. A dark smooth voice suggested her son made the story up. His demented idea of a jealous prank. Emily immediately recoiled and pushed back at the twisted thought.

No! Eric loves me. He wouldn't hurt me. My baby boy would never fabricate a lie this heinous.

"Bad news?"

Robb's whispered question ripped through her panicked thoughts like a sharp knife. Emily opened her eyes again and swallowed hard. She had to play it cool and go out to the lobby without arousing his suspicions. If he was indeed a murderer like Eric claimed, she needed to flee as far away from Robb as possible before he deduced that she left the theater.

"I'm feeling queasy again." She turned to him and winced a little to sell her excuse. "I think I better go to the ladies' room."

Robb flashed a disappointed frown.

"Are you sure you don't want some water? Stay here. I'll go get it. I don't want you to miss the movie."

"That's so sweet of you." Emily touched his arm tenderly to avoid arousing his suspicion. "I won't be gone long. I promise."

"Hope you start feeling better." Robb's lips curled into a renewed smile. "Hurry back."

Emily snatched up her purse. She resisted the urge to also grab her coat. Going outside the theater wearing only a white turtleneck sweater would make her excruciatingly cold. Still, trading comfort for safety was not an option. Emily knew taking the coat would tip Robb off that she did not intend to return to her seat.

She stepped over the sticky patch on the floor and gave him a little wave when she reached the aisle. Robb mirrored her gesture. Emily turned away again and walked at a deliberate pace down the aisle. She pushed back a thick green curtain covering the exit with her hand and stepped through.

"Mom!"

Eric let out a relieved shout when she stepped into the theater lobby. He darted forward from a spot near the concessions counter. She raised a finger to her lips and cast a fearful glance back at the curtain.

"Not so loud, honey." Emily spoke in a hushed tone. "He doesn't know I'm sneaking out of here."

Eric answered with a vigorous nod and threw his arms around Emily. Her son trembled as he embraced his mother. She closed her eyelids and trailed her fingers gently through his hair.

"Let's go home, sweetie, and call the police."

Emily opened her eyes again and held out her hand to Eric. Her son clasped it tight. They started toward the main doors.

"Feeling better I see?"

Mother and son froze simultaneously. Emily's heart raced fast enough that it teetered on exploding at any second. She couldn't tell if her hand trembled or the tremors came from Eric.

"This is too nice of a coat to leave behind at a movie theater," Robb continued. "Luckily I noticed."

Emily dared not turn around and face him. Her attempt to quietly outsmart Robb failed. One frightening question lingered.

Did he intend to murder them as well?

22

E ric silently cursed the moment when Cooper's voice pierced his ears. This plan seemed foolproof in his head but had already begun unraveling before he and his mom reached the movie theater's main entrance. Why couldn't Cooper have stayed on the other side of the curtain for a few extra minutes? They had come so close to getting the head start Eric counted as necessary for surviving the night.

Now he felt like a wild animal trapped inside a cage.

"This isn't what you think." Emily drew a deep breath while keeping her back to him. "I can explain."

"Looks like you're walking out on our date," Cooper said. "But I'll give you the benefit of the doubt. Go ahead. I'm listening."

Give her the benefit of the doubt? Eric bristled at his attempt to deploy the victim card. Anger swallowed his fear for a moment. This asshole murdered Max in cold blood less than two hours earlier. Now he dared to manipulate Emily and send her on a guilt trip? If Cooper hadn't already revealed himself to be an evil son of a bitch, this condescending attitude would have offered conclusive proof to Eric that his mom was out of this loser's league.

"I have a family emergency." She finally turned on her heel and made eye contact again. "I know this kind of torpedoes our plans and I'm sorry. I promise —"

'I'm willing to help if you let me." A palpable irritation threaded through his otherwise polite tone as Cooper interrupted her explanation. "I don't think it's kind to run out without saying anything, do you? Don't you trust me? Do I mean that little to you?"

Eric wheeled around and stared down his assistant principal. His cheeks grew warmer while his eyes flashed with rage.

"She owes you nothing!" he snapped. "You're a murderer! You don't deserve to be in the same room as my mom."

Cooper held the coat belonging to Emily in his arms. He promptly flung it on the floor away from him and took a couple of steps forward.

"Pipe down, you little brat." Cooper jabbed his index finger at Eric. "The adults are talking."

Emily glanced at her coat lying in a heap on the floor and at her date. Her nervous half-frown quickly shifted into an irritated scowl.

"Don't ever talk to my son that way," she said. "Nothing gives you that right."

Cooper's face smoothed again. He forced a smile back on his lips.

"I was totally out of line," he said. "I'm just passionate about you. About us. Look me in the eyes and you'll see. You'll understand."

When Emily met his eyes, Eric witnessed an odd change unfold. Her whole face became a confused, blank slate. She blinked her eyes rapidly and shook her head.

"Wow. I had the weirdest feeling." Emily cast her eyes around the theater lobby and refocused her attention on Cooper a second later. "What are we doing out here? Why is my coat on the floor? We're missing the movie."

He beckoned her toward him, holding out his arms. Emily started forward, intending to follow him back inside the theater. Eric rubbed the nape of his neck and stared at his mom.

What in the hell was she doing?

Shit.

Cooper put her under some kind of hex or spell. Of course! That explained her agitated body language the other night following their allegedly happy date.

"Mom!" Eric seized her arm and wrenched Emily backward. "Stop! Don't go to him."

His mom turned around. Her eyes fell upon him, fixed in a semi-vacant stare.

"He's a good man, Eric. Give him a chance."

Her words felt programmed and robotic even though she said them with a natural cadence.

"No!" Eric snapped his head toward Cooper. "I won't let you kill my mom like you killed my best friend."

His panicked shouts drew the attention of a blonde-haired worker from the concessions counter. Eric recognized her. Ava, a classmate from his fourth period biology class. She left her spot behind the counter and approached Cooper.

"Sir, you're causing a disturbance," she said. "You need to leave the theater before I call the cops."

Cooper folded his arms and turned to face Ava.

"Is that so?" he said. "This doesn't concern you. Go back to serving popcorn and sodas. Mind your own damn business."

The teen crossed her arms as well. She stood her ground and refused to budge.

"Get lost," Ava said. "This is your final warning."

Cooper licked his lips and scowled. He marched directly over to the concessions counter, balled his hand into a fist, and slammed it down through the glass. Ava, Emily, and Eric all unleashed simultaneous screams.

"Jeremy!" Ava called out to another worker at the ticket window. "Call the police!"

Cooper snapped off a large, jagged shard of glass and drew his hand out from the broken case again. His skin didn't bear a single scratch. How was such a thing possible? Eric had seen multiple YouTube videos showing people punching through windows. Their hands were always cut to ribbons by broken glass.

Cooper lunged at Ava.

Ava screamed and sprinted toward the women's restroom, intending to lock herself inside. Cooper proved too quick for the teen. He caught her from behind and slammed the girl's head against the water fountain. Ava fell to the floor. A big gash had opened from her scalp down to her left eyebrow. Fresh blood trickled over her eye and down her cheek.

Eric and Emily dashed forward to restrain him from behind. Cooper thrust an elbow into Eric's abdomen, knocking him backward into his mom. He raised the glass shard above his ear. Ava screamed and flung out her arm while trying to scramble to her feet. Cooper plunged the shard through her right breast. Ava coughed and gagged. Blood dribbled over her bottom lip.

The assistant principal unbuttoned the first two buttons of his shirt, revealing the reaper amulet, and pressed the dark talisman against Ava's forehead. Purple light mirroring what emanated from Max earlier spread from the dying teen into Cooper and spread through his entire body. Cooper closed his eyelids, opened his mouth, and raised his face toward the ceiling.

"Now I am The Crimson Reaper!" he shouted.

Purple light exploded from Cooper's eyes, ears, nostrils, and mouth. A howling wind swept through the theater lobby, passing through Eric like a ghost as he scrambled to his feet. His failure to steal the amulet away from Cooper cost them all in the worst possible way. Christina's warning returned to Eric as though the words still hung fresh in his ears. Whoever unlocked the amulet's full power would gain an ability to wield unparalleled dark magic.

Cooper now owned that power.

"Mom!" Eric tugged on her sleeve as she lay on the ground. "We gotta get out of here. Now!"

Her hand trembled as Emily extended her arm toward him. He pulled his mom to her feet. They turned and made a mad dash for the double entrance doors adjacent to the ticket window. Clicking locks greeted Eric's ears as he reached the doors.

"Where do you two think you're going?"

Cooper's voice turned more menacing and disjointed with a fresh infusion of dark magic into his body. Eric stopped his eyes from wandering back to Cooper. He pressed his hands against the push bar. It refused to budge an inch. No amount of shaking made a difference.

Eric pinched his eyelids shut and let out a frustrated sigh. He needed a miracle or two.

"Our night together can be salvaged." Cooper's tone turned smooth and buttery. "Return to me. Join me at my side. I never intended to rule alone."

Rule alone?

Eric's eyelids snapped open and, at once, he jerked his head toward his mom. A truly horrifying thought struck him and instantly stuck like glue inside his head. That evil bastard's intentions for her grew crystal clear.

Cooper didn't want to murder his mom.

He wanted to steal her soul.

"Don't listen to him," he said. "Don't even look back at him. We'll find a way out of here, somehow."

Emily ran her hands through her hair. Tears trickled down her cheeks as she met Eric's gaze.

"Maybe I can buy us a little time, so you can escape and find a way to defeat him later."

A crease formed in his brow. Eric shook his head. No chance in hell would he leave his mom behind in this place, abandoning her to a grim and dark fate.

"No, mom. I'm not sacrificing you to him. We'll find another way."

Cooper let out an amused chuckle.

"No sacrifices are needed except a minor one," he said. "Submit to my will alone. Your lives will be spared, and we'll become one family."

Eric's hands doubled into fists at his sides. He drew a sharp breath and uncurled his fingers again. Attempting to start a fistfight only promised to end his life on the spot. Then he could do nothing for his mom. Finding a way to outsmart Cooper was his only effective defense. Eric wheeled around, intending to search for a heavy object to ram into the door. Enough brute force should break open the lock or dislodge the door itself and allow him and his mom to flee to safety.

Eric tried to avoid making eye contact with Cooper while scanning the lobby. He failed. What he saw made his blood run cold.

Pure inky blackness devoured each iris and pupil. No trace of whites lingered in his eyes. More unsettling than empty sockets and, worst of all, paired with a menacing smile. A purplish tint coated blood vessels crossing and pulsating beneath the skin on his forehead and cheeks.

An entire face transformed into pure nightmare fuel.

Cooper extended a hand, beckoning them to retreat from the locked doors and come forward. Eric glanced over at his mom. Emily had turned her back to the double doors. A vacant stare returned to her eyes as she met his gaze once again. Her mouth dropped open.

"Mom. Resist him." Eric clasped her forearm as he pleaded with her. "Don't give in to his spell."

She shook his hand off her arm and started forward. Eric silently cursed his lack of preparation. He left the spells from Christina in his car, thinking he'd sneak his mom out of the theater unnoticed. That plan exploded in his face. Now he had no way of stopping Cooper from stealing her away from him — short of tackling and forcibly restraining his own mother.

"Don't go over to him." Eric's voice quavered. "I love you. Please fight the spell."

Her eyes blinked once.

Twice.

Emily finally broke away from Cooper's gaze and looked at Eric again. Confusion and fear reigned on her face. He guided his hand back to his mom and tugged on her forearm.

Panicked voices from moviegoers pierced the dark green curtains covering each entrance from the lobby leading to the screen. Both curtains rustled. Each one drew back a second later, revealing Sheriff Leeds and a deputy. They approached from different sides and held pistols with barrels pointed squarely at Cooper.

"Robb Cooper, you are under arrest." Leeds inched forward, not letting his pistol stray from its target for a second. "Put your hands behind your head and lie face down on the ground."

Cooper's feigned smile evaporated. He kept his back to the sheriff and raised his hands to ear level.

"This isn't a wise move." One of his index fingers twitched like the tail of a cat waiting to pounce. "We all know how this will end. Go back home, hug your family, and forget you ever saw me here."

"I'm not about to walk away from you." Leeds glanced over at his deputy. "Cuff him, Deputy Parks."

Parks lowered his pistol and pulled a pair of handcuffs off his belt. The deputy raised his weapon again and started forward.

A harsh purple light crackled around Cooper's raised fingertips. He clenched his teeth. Eric cast a worried glance at his mom. No chance in hell existed that those handcuffs would ever circle Cooper's wrists. Not with so much powerful magic coursing through his body.

Cooper lowered one arm and flung the limb at Parks. Purple energy discharged from his fingers and enveloped the deputy. Parks' face contorted in agony as he lifted off the floor. Leeds immediately fired his pistol, striking Cooper in the upper spine and skull. A sudden convulsion ripped through his entire frame and the assistant principal tumbled forward. He fell on his face.

Parks did not drop. Still suspended above the floor, violent tremors rippled through his body from head to toe like turbulent ocean waves.

"Here's our chance." Eric tightened his grip on Emily's arm. "Run!"

Cheekbones and jaw bones in Parks' face stretched like rubber. Handcuffs tumbled from his hand. He let out terrified and garbled screams. Both his skin and clothes started melting like an ice cube jammed inside a hot oven. Eric averted his gaze from the dying deputy as they sprinted past Leeds toward the curtain. Pained screams turned to unnatural shrieks. His mom stole a glance at the unfolding carnage. She gagged and pressed a hand tight against her trembling lips. Eric thrust the curtain aside. They sprinted down an aisle straight toward the emergency exit.

More shots rang out from the sheriff's pistol on the other side of the curtain. Leeds let out a loud curse and plunged through the curtain a second later.

"Those were kill shots." Panic threaded through his voice. "He sprang to his feet like nothing hit him and spit out the bullets."

Other moviegoers already fled the theater through the emergency exit. Leeds waved Eric and Emily forward, urging them to keep running.

The curtain melted behind him.

"He's coming this way!" Eric shouted.

All three reached the exit door right as the final remnants of fabric dissolved into an odd green puddle. Cooper strode through the foul-smelling liquid. Green droplets splashed on his socks and the cuffs of his pants. Black eyes zeroed in on the emergency exit.

"I truly wield all power in the universe." Cooper's words were equal parts calm, forceful, and terrifying. "This town — and then this world

— will bow to me."

Eric shoved the door open before they were locked inside again. He braced his shoulder against it while his mom and the sheriff fled through the open doorway. Leeds grabbed him by the arm and pulled Eric outside before the door slammed shut again with extreme force. They found themselves in a narrow alley behind the movie theater.

Leeds let go of Eric's arm and raced over to a nearby dumpster on wheels. He rolled the dumpster in front of the door, temporarily blocking Cooper inside the theater.

"Didn't I order you to stay at your house and lock the doors?" Leeds snapped, turning to face Eric. "Your interference put us all in a dangerous situation here."

Eric jabbed a finger at the sheriff.

"I came here to save my mom," he said. "I wasn't about to let that magic-powered goon have his way with her after what he did to Max."

Emily flashed a brief appreciative smile at Eric. Her eyes hardened when they fell on Leeds.

"This isn't an appropriate time to argue or assign blame," she said. "Robb is still chasing us. We need to go to a safer spot where we'll have an advantage over him."

Leeds gave her a quizzical look.

"Where is this safer spot?"

She cast her eyes at a nearby streetlamp illuminating a part of sidewalk at the other end of the alley. A resolute frown graced her lips. Eric saw within his mom a silent vow to see this battle against Cooper through to the end.

He messed with the wrong family.

"We'll draw him to my house," Emily said. "My daughter-in-law left behind everything we need to combat all sorts of dark magic."

23

Eric sprinted with his mom to his car without looking back to confirm if Cooper had broken through the dumpster barricade. Nothing so simple would restrain him for long since dark magic now flowed through his body unchecked. Eric had never run so hard in his life — not even during a state basketball tournament game going down to the wire. Still, slowing his foot speed was not an acceptable choice if he wanted to stay alive.

They had to reach the car and drive away before Cooper charged out of the movie theater and had a chance to overtake them.

Eric held his mom's hand tight as he ran to make sure she didn't fall behind him. Her breaths grew heavier and shallower by the time they reached the car. She planted hands on hips while he unlocked the passenger door.

"If I knew I'd be running a 100-meter dash tonight, I would have worn better shoes," Emily said.

He yanked open the door and flashed his mom a quick apologetic look. Eric circled around to the other side while she slid into her seat. Emily leaned across the cup holders and unlocked his door. Once he dropped behind the steering wheel, two doors slammed in unison.

Flaming remnants of the dumpster shot like a missile across Eric's peripheral vision as he started the engine. His heart leapt into his throat. Their temporary barricade didn't last long enough against

189

Cooper's power.

Emily snapped her head at him.

"He's headed this way! Drive!"

Eric peeled away from the sidewalk and down Center Street at highway speeds. Angry horns greeted him as he swerved through an intersection and turned down the nearest side street.

"Where are you going?" Emily's eyes followed a row of dimly lit houses. "This isn't the way home."

"I know, Mom." Eric glanced up at his rearview mirror. Did the sheriff reach his cruiser? No signs of Leeds tailing him. "I'm taking a different route. No need to make this easier for Cooper."

He alternated left and right turns down multiple streets. Scattered snowflakes gathered on the windshield. His wipers made quick work of combating the nascent snow shower. Eric only made a final turn down the road leading to their house when he felt satisfied that Cooper was not tracking his car.

Lights were turned on inside both the kitchen and the living room when Eric pulled his car into the driveway and parked.

"Who's in our —"

"Tatiana and Devin stayed behind to gather materials for casting spells," he said, interrupting his mom's worried question. "Christina sent me a bunch of spells that will help us."

Eric unlatched his seatbelt and leaned over the console dividing the front seat. He snatched up the document with all the spells from the back seat and handed it to his mom. She thumbed through the wrinkled pages, lingering a few extra seconds on random spells here and there.

"Will these spells get rid of Robb's magic?" she asked, making eye contact with Eric again.

His thoughts turned to the protection spell and tracking spell from earlier. Both spells failed with a frightening suddenness. Eric understood now that Cooper probably found a way to counteract the spells before he attacked and murdered Max.

"I don't know," Eric said. "I'd feel better about using them if Christina was around leading the charge."

Emily unlatched her seatbelt and stuck the pages inside her purse. A distinct sadness filled her eyes.

"She's not here to save us. It's up to me, you, and your friends to see this through and stop him ourselves."

That's what terrified Eric more than anything else. He wasn't confident anyone inside or outside their house had enough strength or power to stop Cooper from fully executing his plan. They were all inexperienced acrobats performing gravity-defying stunts without a safety net.

Flashing lights accompanied by a siren moved up the street after Eric and his mom exited the car. Leeds also completed his escape from the movie theater. Why was he drawing attention to himself? Cooper would be drawn to the lights and siren and follow him.

Emily shared the same concern.

"What in God's name is he doing?" She stopped at the bottom porch step and stared back at the approaching cruiser. "Sheriff Leeds is a damned fool."

A second cruiser not running flashing lights, or a siren, approached their house from the same direction. Eric exchanged puzzled glances with his mom. Both vehicles drew closer traveling far beyond the posted speed limit. The second closed the gap on the first.

"We better hurry inside." Emily turned and faced the front door. She shivered as she drew out her keys from her purse. "I've got a bad feeling about this."

Eric stepped in front of his mom as she stood before the doorknob, back turned to her while partially shielding her body. His protective instincts kicked in stronger as the siren's wail grew louder. Cooper would not steal his mom from him.

Not tonight.

Not ever.

The siren went silent and screeching tires greeted Eric's ears right as Emily turned the key and flung the front door open. Lights still flashed when the first police cruiser skidded into the bottom of the driveway at an odd angle. At once, a door flew open. Leeds sprang out of the vehicle a moment later.

"I lost him for a while." Heavy breaths escaped the sheriff's lips as he jogged through a mix of fresh and crusted snow toward the porch. "But he's right on my tail again. We better hurry inside."

Emily turned and scowled at Leeds while peering at him from behind Eric's shoulder.

"Why did you run your lights and siren?" She flung her hand at his cruiser. "You basically invited him to follow you here."

Slammed brakes drew all eyes toward the street. The second cruiser skidded to a stop and blocked both cars occupying the driveway. Eric's heart pounded when the driver's side door popped open.

Leeds stepped out, instantly dropped behind the open door, and raised his pistol.

"Step away from them now," he shouted. "I won't let you harm anyone else in my town."

Two sheriffs.

Same face. Same uniform.

Eric's lips trembled, but not from the icy evening air. His entire body stiffened. He screamed internally at his legs, ordering them to move. Neither limb obeyed his commands. Cooper used magic to change his appearance and deceive them with an illusion. Which Leeds was real? Which one was an impostor?

The first Leeds wheeled around to face the second. He also drew out a pistol from his holster and aimed it at his doppelganger's face.

"Who the hell are you trying to fool, buddy?" The first Leeds said. "Your lame magic tricks won't work on me."

Eric's breaths deteriorated into shallow bursts. They looked and sounded like identical twins. His mom nudged his shoulder and signaled for him to join her inside the house.

"Lower your gun," the first Leeds continued. "Lay face down on the snow where I can see you and place your hands behind your head."

Both the second Leeds and his pistol stayed motionless. He pinched his lips together and met his doppelganger with a defiant stare, holding his hunkered down position behind the car door. Neither man flinched while staring the other one down.

"Robb? Please don't do this."

Emily received no answer from calling out his first name. It didn't matter. The version of Leeds closest to their porch kept his back turned away from them but his shoulders shifted. He tensed up as though preventing himself from instinctively glancing back at her and Eric.

Cooper's deception failed. Only a moment. But that's all the time they needed.

"Gotcha," she whispered.

Cooper pivoted around and faced the open front door. Rage surged through both eyes as his face shifted like a lump of flesh-colored sand and coalesced back into its natural form. His sheriff's uniform also morphed back into his original clothing.

"I'm not amused," he seethed.

Shots rang out from Leeds' pistol. Cooper winced and flinched as bullets struck him in the back. He whipped around to the sheriff again and returned fire. Leeds ducked down behind his car door. Fresh holes peppered the frame.

"Enough of this nonsense." Cooper tossed aside the pistol and stretched out a hand. "You've acted as a thorn in my side long enough."

Metal twisted and buckled on the door. It sheared off from the rest of the car and flew across the front yard until colliding with a stout oak tree.

Leeds backpedaled from the airborne door and stumbled. He fell into the snow, landing on his backside. Cooper turned his palm skyward and drew it closer to his face. An invisible force dragged Leeds feet-first across the snow. The sheriff kicked at the air and flailed his arms, trying to impede his movement.

"Lock yourselves inside!" Leeds shouted. "Hurry!"

At once, Cooper's arm shot skyward until his shoulder became level with his cheek. Still lying on his back, Leeds lifted off the ground at an equal rate. His pistol tumbled from his hand. His body zipped uncontrolled through the air like a kite caught in a tornado.

Splat.

Leeds plummeted like a meteor and crashed straight into his windshield. His body twisted so he landed partially on his side. Glass shattered and scattered around the sheriff on impact. Eyes still wide open in frozen terror, Leeds lay amid windshield remnants in an unmoving bruised and bloody heap.

Eric and his mom unleashed simultaneous screams. Emily slammed the door and locked the deadbolt right as Cooper spun around to face them again.

"How do we keep him out of here?"

Panic laced Eric's question and his eyes instinctively darted to his mom like she held the key to this mystery. The protection spell he tried a few hours earlier did not save Max. Doubt over his ability to make any other spells from Christina work properly smothered Eric.

"We'll figure something out."

Emily's attempt to reassure him fell flat. Uncertainty filled her voice and her eyes darted back to the front door quaking on its hinges. Tremors rippled through the frame like a massive earthquake rocked their house from foundation to roof. This was no earthquake.

23

A purple glow enveloped the wood.

It started to melt like candle wax.

"Oh God. He's breaking through the door." Emily backed away toward the stairs. "We've got to find another way to block the entrance."

Tatiana and Devin simultaneously burst out of the kitchen. Concern threaded through their faces.

"We heard a ton of screaming." Tatiana cast a glance at the melting door and drew a sharp breath. Terror filled her eyes. "What's happening out there?"

"Cooper unlocked the amulet's magic." Eric's voice trembled as that revelation departed from his mouth. "He's all-powerful now."

Color drained from Tatiana's face. She pinched her eyelids shut. Devin stared at him in stunned silence. Their reactions encapsulated Eric's own creeping hopelessness. Cooper succeeded in executing his dark schemes, along with every opponent. How long could they delay suffering a seemingly inevitable dark fate?

"We set up protective barriers in a bunch of rooms," Devin said, piercing the growing silence. "I followed the instructions your sister-in-law sent you. Not 100% on all the crystals, but —"

"You gotta be 100%, bro." Eric's eyes fixed on growing chasms in the front door. "He's too powerful for us to make a mistake."

"We're doing our best," Tatiana snapped. "I'm still trying to deal with magic being a real thing."

A thick wood puddle formed in the doorway. The brown liquid flowed in two directions, seeping across the floor and out to the porch. Cooper became visible on the other side. Intense black eyes and a menacing smile greeted them.

"I'm digging these new powers," he said. "I don't know how I lived life any other way."

Chilled air blasted through the open doorway. Emily trembled, but not from a lack of a coat. Her wide eyes trailed a straight line from the front door remnants up to Cooper's face.

"What do you want from us?" Her voice betrayed her fear. "Why are you doing this?"

Cooper shot her a disapproving frown.

"What I want hasn't changed." He held out his hands. "You. Ruling at my side. Give yourself to me. It's the only way forward."

"You can't have my mom." Eric instinctively stepped in front of her to shield her from Cooper. "I won't let you touch her."

Cooper's eyes shifted over to him. His unsettling smile pressed against the corners of his lips, accompanied by a brief chuckle.

"How do you plan to stop me?"

Eric licked his lips and instinctively stepped back as Cooper approached the doorway.

"I don't want to spoil the surprise."

Cooper scoffed at his words and bared his teeth. Veins throbbed in his neck. He started forward, before pausing at the open doorway.

"You should know better than to meddle with powers you can't control." Cooper shook his finger like a club at Eric. "Resist me and I'll destroy you."

Eric pinched his lips together and crossed his arms even as he edged closer to the stairs. Purple energy simmered around Cooper's fingertips. He took two steps forward only to stop again with a violent suddenness.

A visible ripple surged through the open doorway.

Cooper grimaced like he smashed his face against a brick wall. His hands pushed forward. An invisible barrier repelled both limbs. Cooper unleashed a frustrated shout.

Tatiana slid over next to Eric and cracked a smile while staring at their common adversary.

"Surprise," she said.

24

Additional ripples cascaded through the energy barrier preventing Cooper from going inside the house. His fists pounded against open air. As powerless to move forward as a vampire without an invitation to enter. In a way, Eric figured Cooper had transformed himself into a different variety of vampire. The only difference between him and a traditional creature of the night is he feasted on stolen life energy and dark magic instead of blood.

"You think I can't break through a simple protection spell?" Cooper raged. "Magic is infused into every last cell of my body."

He shouted loud enough to draw attention from neighbors on both sides of their street. Eric prayed none walked outside to investigate the commotion. Cooper had stained his hands with far too much blood for one night.

"Hurry!" Tatiana waved to the others in front of the stairs. "Devin and I fixed up a safe room."

Cooper jerked his head over to her. His menacing grin reappeared.

"You can't run. You can't hide. Good luck trying to escape from me."

Tatiana turned away from him and sprinted straight into the kitchen. Eric, Devin, and Emily followed tight on her heels. Salt grains scattered under their feet as they passed through the doorway. Tatiana's eyes shot to the floor and then darted back up to their faces.

"Watch out," she said. "That salt is supposed to keep him out of here."

A thick row of pure sea salt lined the floor at the metal threshold separating the kitchen from the hall leading to Emily's office and the living room. Crystals dangling from mini chains were nailed to the wall. One occupied each corner of the kitchen. Tatiana and Devin went the extra mile to create a protective barrier against dark magic after Eric left the house to rescue his mom. Hopefully, these measures would buy enough time to neutralize the dark magic Cooper drew from the amulet.

"Did Christina send us spells designed to combat the amulet's magic?" Emily asked. "We've already learned guns have no effect on Robb."

Devin's eyes widened.

"You can't shoot him?"

"You can try," Eric said. "It's a waste of time. The sheriff shot him to pieces twice. Bullets did nothing."

"They did nothing?" Tatiana repeated. "How —"

"He spit the bullets out," Emily said, interrupting her. "Fighting magic with magic is our only recourse."

She drew wrinkled pages filled with Christina's spells from her purse and tried to smooth out the paper. Eric's eyes darted from wall to wall a second time. He studied the kitchen, trying to pinpoint any visible weak spots in their protective barriers.

Deafening cracks tore through the room. Tremors shook the walls from floor to ceiling. Everyone pressed their hands to their ears and stumbled to the floor. Eric lifted his chin and searched for the source of the tremors. Sheet rock and wooden beams fractured down the middle of one wall facing the backyard. Paint chips and wood splinters showered the linoleum.

Signs of an earthquake.

Eric knew better.

Cooper was trying to tear down the house. Faced with being stuck outside, he appeared to settle on trapping everyone inside underneath tons of rubble. Eric's heart raced. His eyes darted over to the backdoor. Did they have enough time to reach the backyard before the roof collapsed and pancaked the entire kitchen?

"Is he doing this?" Devin shouted.

Eric shot him a worried look and nodded.

"Without a doubt," he replied. "We gotta stop him."

Walls did not collapse throughout the kitchen like Eric expected. Wood and sheet rock swirled along the fracture like a chunky milkshake in a blender. The fracture widened as each side pulled away from the other. A harsh backlit shadow filled the opening.

Eric's jaw dropped. He had it all wrong.

Cooper was creating a new doorway into the kitchen.

"Where's the sea salt?" Eric's eyes filled with desperation as he looked over at Tatiana. "We need to block him from coming in here."

"On the counter." She pointed to the kitchen island as she scrambled to her feet. "I dumped the rest in a large mixing bowl after spreading salt lines at every doorway."

Tremors receded as the new doorway solidified. Eric sprang to his feet and dashed over to the mixing bowl. His fingers closed around a handful of salt. Eric wheeled around and faced the gaping hole in the wall. Before he took more than a couple steps forward, Cooper darkened the makeshift doorway he created.

"My surprise trumps yours," he sneered.

Tatiana gulped and instantly ducked down behind the kitchen island. Emily joined her. Devin crawled from the dining table toward their position while doing his best not to draw Cooper's attention.

He failed.

Cooper uttered an incantation and swept his hand toward the floor. Linoleum grew sticky underneath Devin's hands and knees. He lifted a hand off the floor. The flooring stretched like melted string cheese and stuck to his skin like fly paper. His limb smacked back down into its former spot.

"Help me!" Devin screamed.

Eric cast his handful of salt at the assistant principal, striking him square in the face. Salt grains scattered across his blackened eyes and cheeks. Cooper matched Devin's screams with an angry guttural shout of his own.

"Mom!" Eric glanced over his shoulder at the island. "Use one of the protection spells. Now!"

Emily belted out an incantation from the list of spells. Every salt grain on Cooper's face glowed. Smoke wafted up from his skin. Flames sprouted beneath the salt, forming visible hollows in his flesh. Cooper swept his forearm across his face in a wild motion, trying to dislodge salt grains burning fresh holes.

Eric sprinted over to Devin and grabbed him by his jacket collar. Fabric tore violently as he hoisted his friend off the floor. Devin let out a pained shout. Large patches of his jeans were still stuck to the linoleum in two spots.

Devin winced, pinched his eyelids shut, and pressed his hands together. Blood dribbled from his palms, down his wrists, and soaked into the cuffs of his jacket. Tears coursed down his cheeks at equal speed. Eric glanced down at the floor again. Patches of skin remained where Devin's hands became stuck earlier.

"I'm so sorry," Eric said. "Hang in there. We'll find a way to fix your hands."

He yanked open a drawer near the kitchen sink and grabbed a couple of dish towels. Eric wrapped the towels around Devin's raw bloodied hands and directed him to a hiding spot behind the island.

"Why are you opposing me?" Cooper shouted.

Eric snapped his head back at their adversary. Cooper got rid of the salt peppering his face at a cost. Ugly pock marks now peppered his skin across his forehead and cheeks.

"You're a murderer," Eric shot back. "No one deserves to be all-powerful — especially you."

Cooper's menacing smile instantly resurfaced. He stabbed an index finger at Eric.

"Brave words for a snotty teen," he said. "Time to put some real fear back in you."

Cooper swirled both hands in the air before him. He raised his head, fixing his eyes on the ceiling, and uttered a new incantation.

timor comedat animum tuum.

Each word hissed from his mouth as though spoken by a sentient serpent. Red mist billowed out from the walls and floor without warning. Eric stiffened like a stone pillar. His eyes widened and his lips trembled.

No. God, no. This wasn't possible.

"How will you oppose me now when I've brought all your worst nightmares to life?" Cooper said, adding a self-satisfied chuckle.

Mist coalesced into the form of a young woman about the same age as Eric. A black gown flowed across her body from her shoulders to her ankles. Brown bordering on black hair fell past her shoulders. Icy blue eyes peered back at Eric and a wicked grin spread across her lips.

Cassandra.

Cooper used his dark magic to bring forth Cassandra.

Eric shot a desperate glance at his mother. Pure terror enveloped Emily's face. Their shared nightmare had been given life — exactly as Cooper promised.

"You're not real," Eric whispered.

He forced himself to look at Cassandra and face her.

"We locked you away," he said in a louder voice. "We buried you where you couldn't be found again."

Cassandra shook her head.

"You'll never rid yourself of me — in life or in death."

The witch glided toward Eric. She towered over him, seemingly floating on an invisible platform suspended a few feet above the floor. His heart raced faster while he backed away from Cassandra. One word spread through his head as her eyes seemingly settled on him alone, smothering every other thought.

Escape.

They had to flee before it grew too late.

Vines sprang forth from surrounding walls and filled the kitchen. Red mist hovered in the room at ankle level. Eric blinked and found himself standing with his mom inside the bedroom at the old Graber house. A bed covered with vines appeared beside them. The cursed plants writhed as they crawled over the bedding.

"Not this again." A tremor threaded through Emily's voice. "God. Please don't let this happen again."

Candles materialized in random spots throughout the room. Flames spontaneously ignited on each wick. His mom's trembling hand still clutched the collected spells Christina sent to Eric. Surely, at least one spell would offer sufficient power to combat a revived Cassandra and banish her again. Eric had to test one out before the awful witch finished what she started six years earlier.

"Your lives rest in my hands." Cassandra stretched out those same hands as she threatened him and Emily. "I rule this house. Everything from the vines to the candles serves my will alone."

Eric and Emily stood frozen in one spot. Neither risked the slightest movement. If any vines sensed their presence, a nightmarish outcome awaited both mother and son. Those green monsters would latch onto their limbs, wrap around each one like tentacles, and drag both victims into fresh cocoons with no escape route.

"Who in the hell are you?"

Tatiana's confused, angry question ripped Eric away from fearful visions of an impending demise. She stood a few steps inside an open doorway. Devin leaned against the wall in the hall behind her with head bent to his chest, still cradling his hands wrapped in dish towels. Thick mist bearing a darkened red hue circled both of Tatiana's ankles.

"Watch out!" Eric's right arm shot forward. He waved her away. "Cassandra is dangerous."

Tatiana gave him a sideways glance.

"More dangerous than Cooper?" she asked. "This is a distraction. An illusion."

"What?" Emily's eyes slid from Cassandra to Tatiana. Disbelief permeated her face. "Honey, I think you're wrong on this one."

"We're still inside your kitchen," Tatiana replied. "Cooper is trying to trick us. Don't believe the illusion."

Darkness engulfed Cassandra's eyes. She ascended toward the ceiling and circled behind them, so she now floated above the bed. Eric felt compelled to turn and meet the witch's gaze.

"I am no illusion."

Her voice devolved into a guttural hiss. Eric's blood chilled in his veins when those words reached his ears. Nothing about her looked or sounded natural.

Cassandra unhinged her lower jaw. Thousands of bugs poured from her open mouth. Spiders. Beetles. Wasps. Ants. Black and red shells covered each individual insect and arachnid. Bugs raced across the floor and crawled over walls on either side as they swept through the room in a tidal wave.

"Bugs." Tatiana's words left her tongue in an alarmed whisper. "I hate bugs."

Eric and Emily finally found the strength and will to move their limbs as the bugs drew closer. They charged toward Tatiana, each grabbing a hand belonging to the terrified teen. All three sprinted through the doorway. Devin jumped to his feet and joined them fleeing down the hall. Bugs sprayed out into the hall on their heels like water gushing violently from a fire hose.

"Is this an illusion?" Eric glanced over at Tatiana. "Everything feels quite fucking real to me."

She gave him an incredulous look.

"Don't you see him watching us run or hear him laughing at us?" she snapped. "Did Cooper make himself invisible to you?"

Eric silently cursed his struggles to combat the dark magic. Tatiana saw through a deception that ensnared him. Cooper vanished from his presence almost as soon as Cassandra appeared on the scene. Did he merely conjure up a shadow version of the witch to trick their minds? Eric thought back to Christina's warnings. Magic drawn from the reaper amulet bestowed power to bend and distort reality.

This hall did not lead to a set of stairs like it used to in the old Graber house. A sharp turn into a second hall followed. Another sudden turn sent them running down a third hall. Vines vanished from the surrounding walls. Dingy gray stone took their place. Lit torches hung suspended from both walls at evenly spaced intervals. All other sources of interior light vanished, swallowed by suffocating shadows.

Cooper compelled them to flee straight into a maze. Or perhaps a dungeon.

Another sudden tremor rippled through the hall in a violent wave. Eric glanced over his shoulder to see if they gained any ground on the horde of insects. No sign of bugs anywhere. They seemingly vanished almost as fast as they first appeared. Their absence did nothing to ease the absolute terror swarming him.

A continuous hum greeted his ears. It grew louder and harsher with each passing second and came from multiple directions. The unpleasant noise reminded Eric of a hummingbird flapping its wings, only distorted in an unnatural way.

His mom gasped.

"What in God's name are those things?"

24

His eyes slid over to Emily. Color drained from her face. Her legs became rooted to the floor like twin tree trunks. Eric stole a glance at both of his friends. Tatiana and Devin trembled from head to toe. Their widened eyes were plastered on the source of the humming. Eric's heart leapt into his throat when he finally forced himself to face the same direction.

Giant winged creatures passed in front of flickering light from the torches. Not quite birds. Beaks and black feathers suggested an avian origin. Scorpion tails and piercing dark human eyes told a much different and more frightening tale.

Even in his worst nightmares, Eric never conjured up such unsettling creatures as the monsters before him.

"This is worse than bugs," Devin said. "Much worse."

Tatiana nodded without looking at him. She backed away from the winged creatures, never taking her eyes off the monsters for a second. One nearest to Tatiana opened its beak and breathed out a menacing hiss matching the one from Cassandra earlier. She answered the creature with a startled scream and stumbled, losing her footing. Tatiana thrust out her arm to brace herself against the wall and keep from falling.

Louder screams from her and Emily followed.

Eric's mouth dropped open. Stones in the wall rippled like the surface of a pond disturbed by a turbulent wind. The wall softened into wet clay and swallowed Tatiana's arm up to her elbow.

"Help me!" Tears rolled down her cheeks. "I'm being pulled inside."

Eric tore his gaze away from his friend and flipped through several pages of spells. Eyes frantically trailed over each word as he sought to preserve her from succumbing to this hellish darkness which Cooper had unleashed upon everyone.

A promising spell grabbed his attention on a page near the back. Eric hoped it would work.

Libera vinctum tuum.

The whole ground shook when he stabbed a finger at the wall and recited the incantation. Tatiana's arm popped free from liquefied stone. She stumbled backward and fell to the floor. Angry hisses from avian monsters flooded the hall. Two swooped toward their intended prey. Tails raised behind each winged creature with massive stingers pointed straight at Eric.

He dipped his chin and flipped back to an earlier page. Eric swung his arm at both oncoming nightmare birds and pressed his fingers together while extending his thumb outward.

Fuge a facie nostra.

Both winged creatures shrieked and vanished in a puff of black smoke. The other nightmare birds followed suit when Eric focused his gaze on each one and repeated the incantation. He let out a relieved sigh and let his arm fall to his side.

These spells worked how they were supposed to work for a change.

"Where are you?" Eric shouted. "Show us your face, you coward."

Dealing with Cooper face-to-face in his super powered state was a preferable option to letting him hide in the shadows while conjured bugs and monsters did all his dirty work. Cooper scoffed at Eric's demand. His laugh echoed like a distant voice bouncing off a canyon wall. His face remained obscured from Eric's vision, no matter which direction he turned.

"You think you can stand against me?" he sneered. "You're one stupid kid. I am a god now. I'll crush you like an ant under my shoe."

Eric hung his head while pondering his next step. What would make Cooper visible? A sudden gasp cut through the walled maze and pierced his thoughts.

Walls quivered like unset gelatin and melted around Eric, his mom, and his friends. Stone blocks turned to black sand and washed over their feet. Flames from fallen torches spilled out across the sand. They sprinted forward trying to avoid being swallowed by a moving floor and pinned helplessly while fire consumed their bodies.

"No! This isn't happening." Genuine fear crept into Cooper's voice for the first time all evening. "How did you find me?"

"The Order of the Crimson Thorns owns this world." A female voice answered him. It sent a chill down Eric's spine. She gave off a dark and cold vibe. "You can't flee to a place where we won't find you."

Eric blinked and suddenly found himself back inside the kitchen. Emily, Tatiana, and Devin all stood beside him near the kitchen island. A thin woman in a black trench coat darkened the makeshift doorway Cooper carved into the wall earlier. Dark hair fell loosely to her shoulders. Fury flashed through her pale green eyes. They hardened into a stony stare while fixing squarely on Cooper backed up against the dining table.

"Your stolen magic belongs to The Order," she said. "I will extract it from you myself until only your rotting corpse remains."

25

Eric hesitated to peel his eyes away from the mysterious woman. Their new visitor and Cooper seemed to possess a deep and intense familiarity with one another. They were adversaries, but Eric didn't trust the woman to be on the correct side of this equation. She gave off a distinct dark vibe that screamed foe rather than friend.

"The Order made me do this, Amy!" Cooper's pitch-black eyes narrowed as he furrowed his brow. "You all forced me down this path. Everything that has transpired is on your heads."

Amy?

She shared the name of Cooper's ex-wife. They knew nothing of her beyond that single nugget.

Eric's eyes shot back to the wall doorway. Inky blackness devoured the pale green in Amy's eyes. The exact darkened hue Cooper possessed. Eric instantly understood how they became a couple.

Two people cut from the same evil cloth.

"If you can stop him, we're all for it," Devin blurted out. He winced as he talked. "Trust me. Nobody here is on Cooper's side.

Amy met him with an icy glare.

"Don't think for a second we are allies," she hissed. "The Order knows what you all did here with your little witch friend six years ago. When I'm done with Robb, I'll deal with you next."

Eric shot an anxious look at his mom. The same fear washed over Emily's face. Yet another adversary for them to conquer.

Cooper clenched his teeth, ignoring everyone else in the room except his former wife.

"You shouldn't have tracked me to Deer Falls," he said. "This will be your final mistake in a long, sad history of mistakes."

He raised his hands above his head. Purple energy crackled at his fingertips. Amy drew back her trench coat and revealed a silver ax at her side.

"I will make an end of you," she said.

Emily tugged at Eric's elbow and motioned toward the wall on the opposite end of the kitchen. He nodded and trailed behind his mom as she crept toward the doorway leading to the front room stairs. Tatiana snatched a large cylindrical shaker filled with sea salt from the counter and then she and Devin quickly followed on their heels.

Purple light illuminated the entire kitchen, stretching across the ceiling like jagged spindly fingers of lightning. A thundering boom reverberated from one end of the room to the other. Amy unleashed a deafening scream resembling a frightening battle cry.

Eric resisted a sudden urge to steal a glance at the chaos unfolding behind him. His mom had the right idea. Flee the kitchen to a safer part of the house. They needed to regroup in a different room and employ stronger protection spells to buy more time to formulate a better plan to defeat Cooper.

When Eric ducked through the doorway behind his mom, walls and floor shifted and distorted like a living kaleidoscope. Walking grew increasingly disorienting as he pressed forward. The stairs grew and expanded until each stair resembled a giant cliff towering over him.

"We can't escape from Cooper." Frustration threaded through Tatiana's voice. "What do we do now?"

Red mist billowed down the stairs. Interior lights all turned black.

Candles appeared out of thin air and sprang to life on every side. Their flames extended from the stairs to the living room in one direction and to Emily's office in the other.

"Oh God," Eric whispered. "She found us again."

Cassandra descended the now-giant staircase, floating from one stair to the next. Her hair fluttered as though battered by an unseen breeze. Icy blue eyes fixed squarely on Eric and his mom.

"You belong to me," she said.

Cassandra's lips curled into a devious smile. Eric's fingers involuntarily wrapped around an object that materialized in his hand. It had a wooden feel. He glanced down. Renewed terror flooded his eyes.

A steak knife with a wooden handle.

Eric's hand trembled. The knife blade slowly rotated inward until the tip pointed straight at his abdomen. He whimpered and tears rolled down his cheeks. His mom's hand came down on his shaking wrist.

"Drop the knife." Emily did her best to speak to him in a soothing tone. "Don't let her control you."

Eric cast a desperate look at his mom. How could he stand against such a powerful witch? He lacked the power to survive in the face of her magic, much less defeat her. If he couldn't stand against Cassandra, then defeating Cooper or Amy also rated as an illogical fantasy.

Why even try?

Why not simply accept his fate and find permanent rest from this nightmarish ordeal?

Divine essence lies within every human. We are all gods in embryo. Everyone can nourish that seed.

Christina's words sprang into his mind while Eric and his mom struggled to stop the advancing blade. The seed she described was woven into his DNA. Memories of Ron and Christina overcoming Cassandra clawed to the surface. Her body dissolving into red mist and spiraling back into the chest flashed before his eyes. Christina possessed the power to defeat this awful witch in the past.

He held the same power in the present.

Eric clenched his jaw and turned his wrist outward until the blade pointed at Cassandra. Her eyes trailed from his wrist up to his face. A confused, angry frown subdued her former smile.

"You are not strong enough to resist me." The witch's tone perfectly matched her expression. "How are you doing this?"

Eric relaxed his hand. The steak knife clattered to the floor and vanished in a puff of red smoke. His eyes trailed back up to Cassandra and he smiled.

"Now I'm going to stick you back inside that chest where you belong."

Still floating, Cassandra drew closer until Eric could reach out and touch her flowing hair if he chose to do so.

"I cannot be bound to a simple chest," she said. "Such a thing is not possible. What a strange and desperate threat to make."

Eric answered the witch with a puzzled look. Memories of Cassandra dissolving and being drawn into an open chest flooded his mind again. She became disembodied after Ron and Christina recited a specific incantation. What he witnessed six years ago made her current boast a total lie. When she was free, Cassandra guarded that chest with a murderous ferocity to prevent herself from being imprisoned again.

Tatiana was right.

He battled a mere illusion. A shadow of Cassandra drawn from his memories and nightmares. The real version remained trapped inside a chest buried deep within the Arapahoe National Forest, never to return. Everything else he experienced in this house — melting walls, hordes of bugs, and scorpion-tailed birds — were also illusions crafted from the worst fears Eric, his mom, and his friends possessed.

Cooper's power to deceive him showed cracks.

"You have no power over me any longer," Eric said. "You cannot control me."

He swept his arm toward Emily, Tatiana, and Devin.

"You cannot control us."

Cassandra unleashed an unholy scream and thrust her arms outward. Tatiana unscrewed the top from the saltshaker and scattered sea salt between Eric and their shadowy foe. Red mist emanating from the witch's hands halted at the salt line. An invisible barrier blocked it from reaching Cassandra's intended targets.

"Know this." Her voice suddenly deepened until she sounded exactly like Cooper. "Your weak efforts to resist my magic will fail. I'll claim your lives and your souls as my property soon enough."

Eric glanced down and flipped through the collected spells again. His thumb stopped on a page containing a previously unused banishment spell. He met Cassandra's gaze again with a confident smile.

From Earth to sky,

hear my words.

Chase this wraith

from our presence.

Forever unable to touch

body, mind, or soul.

When the final word of the incantation passed through Eric's lips, a howling wind tore down the staircase and blasted through Cassandra. She trembled like a leaf and unleashed an anguished scream. Her body dissolved into red mist, vanishing faster than a desert mirage. All traces of mist soon scattered, leaving no sign that the dark illusion which tormented them ever existed.

"Now we strike at Robb directly," Emily said. "Time to end this."

Eric, Tatiana, and Devin each answered his mom with a nod. They must prevail against Cooper. Bring justice to Max, Trace, and his other victims. Become vehicles for their vengeance.

Tatiana cast handfuls of salt ahead of their feet as all four marched back to the kitchen. Fresh confident energy surged through Eric. This no longer loomed as the impossible battle it once seemed. Cooper threw a heavy dose of dark magic in their path, attacking them from many angles, and they all survived.

Now they resolved to take the fight to him.

A chaotic and frightening scene greeted Eric's eyes once he re-entered the kitchen. Broken furniture had been strewn from one end of the room to the other. Giant cracks ran through the windows and walls alike. Glass and ceramic shards were scattered across the floor. Amy's silver ax was partially embedded in the refrigerator door. She and Cooper had carved a path of destruction while battling one another for control of the amulet's magic.

Their battle had not yet reached an end.

"I wish I killed you a few months ago when I had a chance," Amy said. "Things would be much simpler now."

She recited an incantation. At once, a door ripped off one of the kitchen cabinets. Floating wood sheared into multiple pieces. Amy molded the air with her hands. The wood stretched and pulled like wet clay and formed into a series of spears. She swept her arm forward and launched her newly formed lethal arsenal straight at Cooper.

He crossed his arms in front of his face and quickly drew them apart again. Every spear veered off to either side of their intended target. The projectiles struck walls, appliances, and cabinets.

Cooper thrust his arms forward. Purple energy discharged from his hands and flung Amy backward. She slammed against the floor with a hard and loud thud. Linoleum liquefied under her backside. Flooring circled her wrists and ankles, pinning Amy in one spot, and hardened against her limbs.

"I'm going to enjoy every second of torturing you," Cooper said. "You'll beg for me to put you out of your misery long before I'm done."

Amy strained against her restraints and gnashed her teeth at him with the rage of a rabid dog. Cooper circled his ex-wife, matching her fury within his face. Neither one paid visible attention to anyone else inside the room.

Tatiana spread out more salt in a concentrated wide circle around her, Eric, Emily, and Devin halfway between the doorway and the stove. She turned and faced Eric once both ends of the circle connected into an unbroken whole.

"I've done my part," she whispered, trying not to draw Cooper's attention with her words. "Now it's your turn."

Eric pinched his eyelids shut and drew a calming breath. He opened his eyes again a moment later and, together with Emily, scoured through pages of spells. After reading through every page, they backtracked to an incantation near the front. It functioned as a type of banishment spell designed to cast out negative energy. Would it work on simultaneously bleeding dark magic from Cooper and Amy?

Only one way to find out.

"I think we found the right one," Eric whispered.

"Found the right what?"

He stiffened when those four words entered his ears. Eric glanced up from the spell and found Cooper staring at him. His shoes were only an inch or two away from touching the salt circle. Cooper's lips curled into a cunning smile.

"What are you trying to do now?" His tone was equal parts condescending and menacing. "If only you applied yourself in the classroom and on the basketball court with the same vigor."

Eric brushed off his verbal jabs and met Cooper's gaze with a firm stare and resolute frown. They already defeated his illusions. Doing the same thing with this murderous asshole was the next natural step.

"We're not afraid of you anymore," Tatiana said.

Cooper snapped his head over to her and instinctively lunged at Tatiana. An invisible barrier created by the salt kept his arm from reaching the teen. He stepped back and let out a derisive laugh.

25

"Your trite protection spell won't last long," he said. "I'll break down this barrier with ease and end your lives with the snap of my finger."

"It will last as long as it needs to last," Emily said.

Devin and Tatiana drew closer to Eric and his mom. All four started chanting the same words.

Tenebrae te ligant.

iam fugiat.

Magiam tuam abjicimus.

ad umbra regni

Nunquam rediturus.

Cooper's face contorted when the last word fell from their lips. He winced and pressed his hand against his chest. Then the assistant principal doubled over. An anguished groan followed.

"No!" he shouted. "What have you done to me?"

Blackness fled from his eyes and his purple veins receded beneath his skin. Cooper fell to his knees and clasped his hands behind his head. His screams grew louder, soon joined by another voice riddled with pain. Amy writhed on the floor, straining against her restraints, and scrunched up her face. Sweat beaded on her forehead. Blackness also retreated from her eyes.

Streams of dark energy burst from their respective mouths. Purple and black mixed together in the air. A vortex opened in the kitchen floor. Magical essence drawn from Cooper and Amy spiraled downward until it all vanished through the vortex. The hole sealed again once the last trace had been consumed.

"I feel empty." Amy panted and sank back to the floor. "How did you —"

"Simple banishment spell," Emily said. "You and Robb are empty soda cans. Not one ounce of magic is left in either of you."

"Please don't do this," Cooper pleaded. "We can make this work. I will be your god and you will be my goddess."

Emily gave him a look that would melt ice.

"The last man who told me something like that also turned out to be a no-good lying bastard."

Amy pushed against her restraints with a burst of renewed vigor.

"You want her to be your goddess?" she snapped. "Do I mean nothing to you?"

Cooper unloaded an angry sigh and scrambled to his feet. He ripped out a wooden spear stuck in the wall nearest to him. Amy's eyes filled with terror as she realized what he intended to do. Her lips trembled as Cooper marched over to his ex-wife. With one fluid motion, he brought his arm down and drove the spear tip through her mouth.

"You did this to me," he said. "You forced me down this path."

The spear pinned Amy's head to the floor. She gagged up blood and convulsed for a moment before becoming permanently still.

Even without dark magic flowing through his veins, Cooper proved he was still the same old sadistic murderer. They could not let him escape their grasp.

"Call 911!" Tatiana shouted.

Rage filled his eyes as Cooper wheeled around. He snatched a broken chair leg off the ground and charged toward her. Devin and Eric slid in front of Tatiana. Cooper jumped across the salt line and blasted Devin square in the jaw with the broken end. His blow sent the teen tumbling backward. Devin collided hard with the floor and let out a pained groan.

Eric countered with a right hook to Cooper's nose. Tatiana scooped up salt from the ground and darted forward. She tossed salt in his eyes. Cooper screamed and recoiled. He yelled an unintelligible word at both teens. Eric ripped open a drawer and fished out a long utility knife. Tatiana dropped back behind him and whipped out her smartphone, intending to call the police.

Cooper jabbed the broken chair leg at Eric's chest. Eric narrowly avoided getting struck like Devin. He held the utility knife out in front of him, blade pointed straight at the assistant principal.

"You haven't beaten me," Cooper raged. "You're only a bug on my windshield and I will crush you."

He swiped at Eric a second time. Eric kept backing away, never lowering the knife for a second. Cooper pushed forward until he backed Eric up against the pantry door.

Cooper raised his left arm, intending to club Eric with the broken chair leg until he bled out. He let out a violent scream a second later.

His arm fell to the floor.

Blood gushed out from inside his torn coat sleeve.

Eric refocused his gaze from Cooper's face, now contorted in pure agony, and slid his eyes past his shoulder. His mom had circled around the kitchen island unseen and stood behind Cooper. Both hands gripped the silver ax that belonged to Amy. Fresh blood smeared across the sharp blade. A long narrow hole lingered like a scar in the refrigerator door.

Cooper swung around and staggered toward Emily, stretching out his other intact arm.

"Please spare me," he pleaded, wincing as he spoke. "I'll do whatever you want."

"I want you to join your ex-wife," Emily said.

She swung the ax a second time and drove the blade deep into his face. Blood spurted out as flesh parted along both sides of the ax. Cooper lurched forward and collapsed unmoving on the kitchen floor in a growing puddle of his own blood.

Eric dropped the knife and muttered "thank you" to his mom. Emily stepped over the fresh corpse and shared a relieved hug with her son. Tatiana quickly joined their embrace.

Sirens wailed outside the house, growing louder with each passing second. Eric wondered how they would explain the scene of carnage inside the kitchen and outside the house to whichever deputies arrived on scene. Figuring out those details was a secondary concern.

Right now, he simply wanted to savor their victory.

A distinct feeling of peace washed over Eric as he pulled back from hugging his mom and Tatiana. Together, they stopped a brutal serial killer from ruling the whole world as a self-proclaimed god. Everyone Cooper slaughtered to obtain his dark magic could now find rest for their souls.

26

Eric hesitated to remove the reaper amulet from Cooper's lifeless body at first. Would merely touching or handling the cursed talisman infect him with dark magic? One look at the other exhausted faces inside the room overrode Eric's latent fears. The reaper amulet destroyed countless lives by inspiring one evil man's murderous rampage through Deer Falls. No other path lay before him than taking the amulet and erasing it from existence.

"We can't let anyone else discover this thing." Eric lifted it up and over Cooper's head. "It's too dangerous."

He concealed the amulet inside his coat when new sets of flashing lights appeared outside the kitchen window. No one breathed a word about it while in the presence of deputies who responded to Tatiana's 911 call. They arrived at the house about five minutes after Cooper took his final breath.

Paramedics were already trudging across the front yard when Emily opened the front door. An ambulance and two police cruisers blocked the street. Eric peered over his mom's shoulder at the vehicles. One deputy approached Leeds' car. She broke down and cried upon seeing his lifeless body splayed amid a broken windshield. The other deputy tried to comfort her while battling his own visible grief.

"My friend is badly hurt," Tatiana said, beckoning to the paramedics. "He needs to go to a hospital."

Emily and Eric both stepped aside to allow enough room for a stretcher to roll past them. Tatiana led the paramedics inside the kitchen to Devin. Both deputies continued toward the front porch once they regained their composure. Emily beckoned them forward.

She took a cautious approach when the two deputies peppered her with questions about all the events that unfolded earlier in the evening. Eric took note of his mom's efforts to omit any information connecting their experiences and survival to magic in her answers. He wasn't sure either deputy believed Emily's story, judging by their bewildered expressions, but they simply jotted down a few notes and then promised to follow up with additional questions later.

Devin was taken away in the ambulance, still alive and conscious. He gave Eric a thumbs up and flashed him a pained smile as paramedics rolled his stretcher past the front door. Tatiana left the house a few minutes after the ambulance drove away. She called her parents before leaving for home to let them know she was safe and tearfully told them how much she loved them before ending the call.

The two deputies cordoned off the kitchen with yellow police tape and lingered long enough to help Emily and Eric pack overnight bags. They had to stay elsewhere until all forensic evidence had been collected inside and outside the house.

An uncomfortable silence settled inside his mom's car after Eric tossed their overnight bags in the backseat and climbed into the passenger seat. Emily opened the garage door, but then sat behind the steering wheel staring straight ahead without starting the engine.

"What did he do … to you?"

Eric posed his question with some hesitation. Cooper used his magic to briefly gain control over her mind at the movie theater. Seeing the troubled look in her eyes now, Eric realized with a grim sadness it wasn't the first time that bastard assaulted his mom in that fashion.

"He violated me in an unthinkable and unforgivable way." Emily pinched her eyelids shut and dipped her chin to her chest. "Memories I didn't know existed flooded back to me after Robb lost his magic."

"Memories? What memories?"

"He murdered someone before my eyes and stripped memories of what I witnessed from my mind."

Eric stared at her in stunned silence. His mom had been as much of a victim of Cooper's unchecked thirst for power as anyone he murdered.

'When I close my eyes, my thoughts drift to how Robb stole my mind and tried to steal my soul." Tears rolled down Emily's cheeks when she opened her eyes again. "I know he's dead, but I'm still afraid."

"Thank God, he can't hurt you now, Mom." Eric said, trying to reassure her. "You're beyond his reach."

"Am I?" She tilted her head at him and brushed away tears. "What if Robb rises from the dead? Or returns to torment me as a ghost? Living in a world where magic is real, I don't feel like I'm ever beyond his reach."

Eric reached inside his coat and pulled out the reaper amulet. Anger welled up inside of him as he studied the talisman. A piece of mystical jewelry that sowed pain, suffering, and death for too many innocent people. It only existed as a conduit for dark people to obtain power they didn't deserve to wield. If the reaper amulet remained intact, another monster like Cooper would inevitably arise to claim ownership and channel its cursed magic into their bodies.

His eyes slid over to his mom. Eric let the amulet fall into his lap while reaching out and embracing Emily.

"I love you," he whispered to her. "I'll do my part to keep you safe from the likes of Cooper as long as I live."

Emily offered up a grateful smile when Eric pulled away again and settled back into his seat. She started the engine and backed the car out of the driveway.

* * *

Getting rid of the reaper amulet turned out easier than Eric expected. He called up Christina a day after they slew Cooper and she hunted down detailed instructions on how to destroy the cursed talisman. Emily jotted down careful notes and helped Eric perform the proper ceremony at sunset.

Mother and son crushed gemstones once embedded in the odd-shaped cross into a fine powder and melted surrounding metal into a silvery liquid. Then Eric recited an incantation designed to prevent the amulet from being molded a second time. They scattered all remnants across the same part of forest deep within Nickel Canyon where Ron and Christina permanently buried Cassandra's chest.

Peace washed over Eric when his mom drove them down the canyon back to Deer Falls. For the first time, he truly believed they had gained an upper hand over the darkness infesting that town.

One frustration remained for Eric.

Their role in saving Deer Falls and the rest of the world from Cooper's machinations went unnoticed. Part of that ignorance was created by design. Both he and his ex-wife seemed to be affiliated with an evil clandestine organization. For that reason, Emily thought it prudent to not draw undue attention to themselves. She urged Eric, Tatiana, and Devin to keep the true version of events surrounding Cooper's death a closely guarded secret. Stay silent and let Deer Falls community leaders fabricate their usual cover story. With luck, what they said publicly would steer the so-called Order of the Crimson Thorns down a different path.

Tatiana shared his frustration.

She showed up at Eric's house on the first Saturday after Deer Falls lost in the state basketball playoffs. An agitated frown graced her lips when Tatiana stepped out of her car and walked up the driveway. She tried to hide her sour feelings when Eric opened the front door and stepped out onto the front porch.

They spilled out anyway after the two friends shared a lingering embrace.

"I finally understand what you must have felt after what happened to you six years ago," she said, pulling back and meeting his gaze. "Anger. Sadness. Frustration. How do you cope?"

Eric paused while he mulled over how to answer her question. Truth be told, coping well with trauma was not his strong point. It took every ounce of inner strength he owned not to lose his mind after what Cassandra did to him and his mom. Healing from deeper scars Robb Cooper left in his wake would require a greater dose of mental fortitude.

"You fight to survive," he finally said. "That's the best anyone can do in our situation."

Tatiana turned away from him. Her eyes settled on his house. Repairs drawn out over several weeks restored the place close to how it appeared before Cooper carved a winding path of destruction from one end of the kitchen to the other. Contractors filled in the door-sized hole in one kitchen wall. Melted flooring and walls were rebuilt or replaced.

After she studied the house for a moment, Tatiana's eyes slid back to Eric, and she turned to face him again.

"You're truly leaving for good, aren't you?"

Eric looked down and away. He licked his lips and finally answered her with a reluctant nod.

"Mom and I both need a fresh start. Too many brushes with death in Deer Falls. Doesn't add up to a happy future if we stay here."

His eyes trailed over to the mailbox. A brand new for sale sign occupied an adjacent spot in the grass only a few yards away. Emily showed no reluctance about putting it up this time around.

Eric clasped Tatiana's hand and met her gaze again.

"I wish you could leave with me."

Her lips curled into a regretful smile. Eric knew his wish wasn't possible. Not with both her parents clinging to the skeptical mindset Tatiana embraced before everything that happened with Cooper.

"I'll meet you." She gave his hand a gentle squeeze. "Graduation isn't far off. Neither is 18."

Tatiana drew closer. Eric also leaned forward as she tilted her head. His hand circled behind her back. Their lips pressed together in a wet passionate kiss.

Her smile deepened when Eric's lips retreated from hers again and he gazed into her eyes. He loved Tatiana with a depth that surprised him. It took the prospect of being separated from her for him to accept and embrace the true feelings he tried to bury all this time.

"I'll be waiting for you," Eric said.

No new life beyond the horrors of Deer Falls would feel complete without her in the picture.

THE END

About the Author

Being a storyteller is second nature to John Coon. Ever since John typed up his first stories on his parents' typewriter at age 12, he's possessed a thirst for creating stories and sharing them with others. John graduated from the University of Utah in 2004 and has carved out a successful career as an author and journalist since that time. His byline has appeared in dozens of major publications across the world.

John has published several popular novels, including the *Alien People Chronicles* trilogy. His debut novel, *Pandora Reborn*, became an international bestseller on Amazon and ranked as the no. 1 horror novel in Japan for a brief time. His novel *Alien People* earned distinction as a Top 100 new release and Top 100 bestseller in multiple science fiction categories on Amazon.

John lives in Sandy, Utah. Bookmark his official author website (johncoon.net) for news and updates on his fiction. Subscribe to his newsletter, Strange New Worlds (http://johncoon.net/subscribe) to receive original short fiction, poems, and articles.

Also by John Coon

Check out these other captivating stories from author John Coon available through Samak Press.

Pandora Reborn

A buried chest is unearthed and opened, bringing forth an ancient witch who terrorizes Deer Falls. Can Ron Olson and his new friends stop her before she destroys them and the small Colorado town?

The first book in the *Deer Falls* horror series.

Snow Dragon

A mythical monster has awakened beneath Deer Falls following a major earthquake. Can the Duggan family destroy this vicious and lethal predator before it drives their sleepy Colorado town to extinction?

A monster horror novella and a prequel to the *Deer Falls* horror series.

Alien People

Discovering a distant probe bearing a message of peace inspires alien explorers to journey to a mysterious planet called Earth. Will first contact bring new understanding … or take a deadly turn?

The first book in the *Alien People Chronicles* science fiction adventure series.

Dark Metamorphosis

A brutal abduction reveals a dark conspiracy to destroy all survivors of the Earth expedition. Can they fight deceit and evade assassins to reveal the dreadful truth?

The second book in the *Alien People Chronicles* science fiction adventure series.

Among Hidden Stars

A tyrannical ruler seeks an ancient relic that imparts god-like powers to use as a world-conquering weapon. Will a rebel couple find the hidden relic first and finally defeat their oppressor's reign?

The third book in the *Alien People Chronicles* science fiction adventure series.

Under a Fallen Sun

A Texas town has fallen under siege from an alien menace. Four college students are trapped inside the small town, battling for their lives. Can they defeat these invaders who seek to conquer Earth?

A science fiction novel set in the *Alien People Chronicles* universe.

Hollow Planet

A barren planet holds a startling secret tied to its distant past. Will uncovering evidence of an ancient alien race forge a new alliance? Or will discovery exact a deadly cost for these explorers?

A science fiction novella set in the *Alien People Chronicles* universe.

In Hell's Shadow

Trapped in an unfamiliar place far from home after an accident, Kate must confront a once buried nightmare anew. Will this dark secret from her past lead her to certain destruction?

A paranormal horror short story set in the *Deer Falls* universe.

Hiding From Shadows

Every night is a personal battle to survive until morning for Ellen. An unseen menace lurks in the shadows outside her home. Will it strike without mercy once she lets her guard down?

A paranormal horror short story set in the *Deer Falls* universe.

www.ingramcontent.com/pod-product-compliance
Lightning Source LLC
Chambersburg PA
CBHW061523310726
48972CB00008B/2312